THE INAMORTA

THE INAMORTA
or, *Death's Beloved*

Joshua Rex

Trade Paperback Edition

Text © 2022 by Joshua Rex
Cover and interior art © 2022 by Nick Greenwood

All persons, places and organizations in this book—save those clearly in the public domain—are fictitious, and any resemblance to actual persons, places or organizations living, dead or defunct, is purely coincidental.

Editor & Publisher, Joe Morey
Co-editor, S. T. Joshi

Copy editing and book design by F. J. Bergmann

ISBN: 978-1-957121-10-9

Weird House Press
Central Point, OR 97502
www.weirdhousepress.com
Join the Weird House mailing list at our website!

This book is dedicated in loving memory of

ANNE O'BRIEN RICE

"It's really about us."

16th November, 1799
Journeying to Teethsgate

I have never been one for journal-keeping. The singular art of the disciplined diarist is not within the scope of my abilities, nor interest for that matter. However, the recent nightmares, coupled with the lack of anything exterior to divert my thoughts from the horrific visions, have prompted me to begin recording my daily experiences in the hopes that through writing them I might obtain some transitory respite, and perhaps even gain insight as to the source of these recurring terrors.

The events of the dream are invariably as follows: I am running from something through a dark and cloistered passageway—most likely a catacomb, though I never encounter any bones. The *smell* is certainly charnel, emanating from both the many ramifications as well as the rapacious thing which pursues me. Though I have not seen it, I nonetheless have an image in mind of the nature and characteristics of the creature. There is the half-run, half-trot of something unaccustomed to moving on two legs; the white and scabrous hide stretched over a frame of grotesquely formed bone; the slackened maw with its muddle of barbed and blunted teeth. But most unnerving without question are the eyes—dull and sightless as the coins placed over those of the dead. Ultimately and invariably I am overtaken, brought down with its jaws on my neck, and as I strike the fetid floor, I am jolted awake in the carriage.

This has been the way of it for each of the three nights since our departure from his Majesty's court, and now this afternoon, after a repugnant meal of jacket potatoes and "roast meat" at a ramshackle roadside tavern, followed by a post-prandial vomiting of hot red mush into the soupy mud, the dream began in plain daylight as I lolled half-conscious in the joggling cabin. Of course I have *never* slept well in coaches; even after a decade of transcontinental journeys, the prospect of uninterrupted and satisfactory rest is one of exasperating inscrutability. Most nights I find myself glaring through the gloom at my father, for whom sleep has never proved so elusive. As I write this he is snoring in his corner, short periwig askew, a small book lying cover-side down on one leg and his gold-tipped cane resting against the other. He has been slumbering often of late since developing croup a fortnight ago. Presently, the sour and faintly alliaceous reek of the moss-green tincture he imbibes as treatment pervades our little box on wheels, and is threatening to rouse my suppressed nausea. And so, in the interest of distracting myself from the queasiness and ennui, I shall chronicle not only the dreams, but the details of this most recent miserable expedition.

For the last several days we have been traversing a dismal and tenebrous wood. The vista is a monotony of black bark and forest scrub. Moonlight cuts crooked figures from the shadows and sets them capering on shard-like appendages amidst the deadfalls. More harrowing than these is the phantom reflected back at me in the diminutive rectangular pane: the raddled apparition with thinning yellow-white hair and sunken eyes and the liver-tinted patch that stretches from left cheek to collarbone. In sum, these belie a young man of twenty-one years. What he longs for is the continuity of a bed and a home, and he is quite envious of the viola resting beside him in the dark velvet of its wood and leather shell.

The root snagged path has at last ended, delivering us onto a rolling plain of harvested wheat stubble. I reckon we are nearing our destination, for the sea is visible in the west—a grey wrinkled blanket surmounted by smoky cloud-lather dragging squall tendrils. The weather has been insufferably damp inland, and it appears there will be no reprieve from it here. I spy as well an ancient village of stone buildings with steeply gabled roofs standing like a tight cluster of megaliths before a sallow harbor. My father previously mentioned to me the name of this place; I cannot recall it now and suppose that it does not matter, as this is to be a comparably brief stay. Typically we would not venture to such hinterlands for any fee, but the private commissioning of a sonata in three parts by Rufus Canis, the ostensible Count of this region, was indisputably too lucrative to refuse. (I should add that the commissioned composition was completed just prior to departing the royal palace, and henceforth will require only a few days' rehearsal, for my father's sake, before Friday's performance.) I pause to reëxamine the invitation. The rare indigo parchment and the silver and gold script written thereupon in an archaic and stately hand reflect indeed a local lord of extreme wealth.

We have entered the village and are riding along its cobbled main thoroughfare. It is a forlorn hamlet of ivy-trussed houses mottled with lichen and black mold. The rain-streaked casements and dormers are begrimed, and nearly all are shade-drawn. The town square is a silent aggregate of shops squatting along the derelict waterfront; their painted signs are faded and salt-stripped. The inner harbor is visible through breaks between the buildings. I see glimpses of a dilapidated pier and ten or so rancid fishing trawlers bound to rotted dock pilings near the scummy shore. The village's air of despondency seems shared by the handful of individuals moving hurriedly along the weedy slate walkways, faces downcast, weary of one another as they are of us.

Skirting the eastern extremity of the harbor, the road has abruptly become an incline so sharp and perpetual it has brought us into a band of low-lying fog. The occlusion of view is total; as I look back through the rear window for bearing, I find the shore and village shrouded by this dense winding sheet of mist. I am startled by a sound: a disembodied chorus of moans in octave. The wind buffeting the coach? Despite the vertiginous pitch of our climb and the blind ascent, we seem incongruously to be picking up speed.

We are now upon a plateau-like summit where the narrow way rims the edge of a sheer descent of one hundred or more yards to angry breakers and slick boulders below. Rogue gusts shake the cabin, causing it to rock pendulum-like toward the brink and back again. Another surge of nausea grips me—I must shut my eyes....

To my supreme relief, the road has cut away from the cliff face, and we are headed in the direction of the verge of an immense forest. Just now, I see what must be our destination, though it appears decidedly less opulent than reputed: a modest white keep, flanked by a pair of towers with blue conical caps. Brilliant tangerine pennants flap like lizard tongues from their twin spires. The façade is windowless, save for a single burnt-orange lancet set at the center of the castle, situated above a pair of black double doors.

My father has woken and is regarding the castle with the same bewilderment as myself. Our coachman is unloading our trunks, and the horses are becoming anxious as the squall drifts nearer; still no servants have emerged from the entrance. Here, then, I shall pause until we have determined what to do next.

16th November 1799
Late Evening, The house of Rufus Canis

The timing of the commencement of this narrative was fortuitous, as it now affords me a means in which I might detail the grandiose and frequently grotesque particulars of the Count, his house, and his family. These last several hours have been unequivocally the most bizarre that we have passed as guests in the residences of royalty or otherwise. In order to obtain a thorough estimation of what I have seen and experienced, I believe it is essential to detail all of the events from our first encounter. I shall therefore begin this singular exposé at the moment that we disembarked from the carriage.

"Perhaps they did not see us approach," my father said. He had one arm locked around mine, while his cane bore the balance of his considerable weight. There had been no response to my first nor my second set of raps upon the great arched doors. I glanced back at the carriage, which was already disappearing back into the fog, then beyond at the thunderheads moving rapidly inland. I was dismally considering the forest as a temporary shelter when the doors were unbolted and four porters, elegantly coiffed and clad in tailcoats and breeches, descended the stairs and began gathering our things. One of these dull-eyed drudges audaciously reached for my instrument case but I rebuffed his attempt. In retrospect, I believe that I actually growled at him! A fifth man standing on the threshold bade us wordlessly with a vague wave to follow him inside.

Upon entering the castle, it took several moments for me to comprehend my surroundings, for I was standing within a cube of infinite reflection: the walls, floor, and ceiling were all mirrors, lit by scores of girandoles whose tiny multiplied flames seemed in sum bright as a conflagration. The servant went on ahead, accompanied by an army of likenesses, and opened a panel in the far wall. Through this a regal and resplendently dressed man stepped through.

My first impression of Rufus Canis, "Count of the Westvold," as he introduced himself, was one of discordance. In dress, he was exceedingly old-fashioned, his clothing being the style of a century earlier. Besides the high and powdered peruke, his bronze knee-length coat was pleated, buttoned to the hem, and silver-embroidered. His hose were the same shade as the embroidery, and the buckles of his umber suede shoes gleamed with diamond light. Inconsistent with this was his boisterous manner, youthful parget-pale face, and lucid sunset-yellow eyes, which glanced often at my instrument case.

"At last, the *maestros* Layne! We have awaited your arrival with great anticipation," he boomed. "I hope your long journey was uneventful?"

We replied that it had been so as he shook our hands with such fervor and cheer we felt ourselves obliged to humor him with candid expressions of our appreciation for the great generosity of his commission.

After salutations, he led us through the outlandish foyer and into a cavernous hall of pure white marble with a towering rib-vaulted ceiling. Between these curving ribs rising to the apex were massive inlaid mirrors like a ring of fangs. I gasped, a sound reiterated by my father which in turn was met with a pleased chortle from our host. The space was lit by several hundred petite orbs balanced on ornate crystal sconces set along the walls and glowing astral-like along the inwardly curving heights. The source of their illumination continues to confound me. They are without flame or chimney, and yet the swirling, cloudy mass not only shines with a flameless luminescence, but emits a low and wavering hum. In regarding them, I pondered whether they were a progression of de la Rue's platinum-filament incandescent lamp. The combined sound of these was that of a mournful vesper, though so hushed and tenuous no specific melody could be discerned. Two yawning corridors of equal grandeur, though smaller in scale, stretched to the right and left of the central hall. There were two colonnades on either side of the second level; colonnades of bloodless caryatids with curiously gaping mouths formed the supports between the arches. Along the rear wall was a pair of doors with figures carved in high relief. A crisscrossing staircase led to a similar set of doors which accessed the second level. Curiously, I saw a third entrance floating above the latter—a small and unremarkable board-and-batten lancet, which the stairs did not lead to and was accessible by no means that I could perceive. The Count espied me regarding this and said:

"It is an old house, throughout which you will find many such anomalies. The aspirations for our desired augmentations are, alas, regrettably curtailed by the limited aptitude of our regional artisans...."

I intended to inquire as to how the covering-up of a single door should exceed in difficulty the placement of those fanged mirrors, but the Count had already began detailing for my father in an exhausting and rather circumlocutory manner a comprehensive and date-oriented account of the castle, its construction, and the ancestors who built it. The House of Canis, it seems, has genealogical roots in the Westvold going back five centuries, when the village of Larmes Harbor was called Lychton. It, along with the other coastal ports of the region, was captured by Falsus Canis, who built Teethsgate to serve as both his home and a defensive stronghold against hordes of marauding barbarians who once dwelled in the sprawling woodland that extends from the coast to several hundred miles inland.

The Count's lecture was disrupted by one of my father's coughing fits; the stertorous noise echoed cacophonously and indeed frightfully in the vast interior. Our host's countenance turned much alarmed at this display, and he insisted that we get my father to his suite at once where he might repose.

We proceeded from the great room to the long passage on the right. Concerning this, two details were disquieting. First, the space through which we traveled seemed to sweep past us more rapidly than we ourselves moved. The only rationalization I could formulate for this was fatigue, which I was indeed heavy with. Second, there was only a single portal along the entire corridor. It was flanked by a pair of servants whom I initially mistook for statues, so still did they stand. They gave no indication or acknowledgment of us as we approached the door. I felt disarmingly faint by the time we reached it, a sensation which did not disperse until several moments after the Count brought us through the doorway and into the narrow yet lofty chamber which was to serve as my father's quarters.

It was as if they had lifted his ideal image of such a place directly from his mind. There was another gasp, this one from the old man as he surveyed the seemingly infinite number of volumes filling the shelves that lined the walls from barrel ceiling to entryway landing. Proceeding from the latter was a shallow set of steps leading to a recessed area covered in honey-toned rugs, and where stood a gaudy curlicued pianoforte, a study table and secretary desk of similar grotesquerie, and a sumptuous bed with its headboard partly recessed within a pointed stone arch.

As I assisted him down the brief flight of stairs my father requested to be taken to the study table, where stood tantalizing piles of finely bound books; I guided him instead to the bed. He broke into another spate of coughing as I helped him up and lifted his legs onto the silken coverlet. So weak was he that I had to get the bottle of tincture from his coat pocket, uncap it and bring it to his lips. He sipped the pungent stuff slowly, allowing only a slight dribble down one cheek which I directly dispensed of with my own handkerchief. I knew that he was much humiliated to appear in such a pathetic state before the Count, but the latter, for his part, showed nothing but perfect sympathy for the old man's condition, and requested several times before he and I departed the room if there was anything he might do to make "the master more comfortable." My father stated that the Count had already been most gracious in the furnishing of such an exemplary lodging, and that he was eager indeed to begin perusing the titles of that unending collection.

"I have planned a banquet in honor of your arrival," the Count said. "The Countess and I would be much obliged if you would join us this evening, should you feel sufficiently rested, *maestro* Jonas, and you, *maestro* Theodore, sufficiently recovered."

"Certainly, my lord. I assure you this is but a transitory grippe," my father replied.

"I shall come for you later, Father," I called out as the Count and I turned to depart. I cannot say precisely why, but I felt apprehensive about leaving him there—beset, as it were, by a portentous melancholy. Perhaps it was due to the suspicion I have that this most recent illness is more sinister and virulent than we are aware, or maybe it was because we had not parted company in several days for any span longer than a few minutes. I suppose my father and I have become strongly accustomed to one another, like a man and his old dog. As the door was closing I glanced back for a reassuring parting look, but found him already snoring on his ostentatious pillows.

We returned to the stair hall, where I followed the Count up the crisscrossing stair toward the upper set of double doors, which were similarly flanked by another pair of servants. The figures carved into these oaken slabs were not the usual rank of ascetic monks and imperial sovereigns soberly proclaiming their divine right, but rather a disparate aggregate of impish half-beasts roiling and snarling in their stacked rows. Such violence! Such obscenity! Their vulgar postures and the depictions of their lewd and murderous acts were of such unspeakably inventive depravity that I dare not record them herein lest they irreparably taint this manuscript. Observing my extreme horror and disgust, the Count, to my surprise, chortled again, and then articulated something which I cannot recall verbatim concerning refinement and elegance and how often they germinate from that which is wretched and cruel.

Entering the second level, I anticipated another grand view but was met instead with a plain stone corridor with a low ceiling and a single opening through which a polished but unadorned stair rose up and out of view. The Count escorted me left, then left again across the colonnade spanning the arch high above the ochre and white fang-patterned floor of the stair hall, and then once more left, where we passed a simple door akin to the one floating above the zigzagging staircase, with an inverted torch on either side whose "flames" were more of those mysterious illuminated baubles. No guards stood here, though some were present up ahead at the massive archivolt-crowned portal. As we drew near, they became animated, moving perfunctorily to open the doors.

The chamber beyond was palatial, ringed in marble galleries, and featured the cyclopean amber-paned lancet I had first glimpsed during our approach. I was mesmerized by the crimson silk trappings and the magisterial and almost comical proportions of the appurtenances (the canopied bed could have comfortably accommodated a dozen individuals) but as well perplexed, for surely this was the solar of the Countess and the Count. I was thus doubly shocked when the latter indicated that this would be my quarters for the duration of our time at Teethsgate. The Count then inquired whether I found it acceptable, to which I replied that it was of course superlative—a reaction which seemed to please him exceedingly. At this he took his leave, reiterating the occasion of the evening's banquet before exiting.

I walked throughout the apartment, scanning its staggeringly massive furnishings. I thought about napping, but now that I had both time and a bed, I found myself irritatingly restless. My trunk had already been delivered; it stood dwarfed by a gigantic armoire that made it look like a vanity trinket box in comparison. I got from it a clean black suit and cravat, and the third movement of the commission which I had decided to annotate with performance remarks for my father. I put the suit on and took the pages to the fireplace. Two wingback chairs stood before the hearth. There was a small table between them, upon which stood a decanter of sherry and a single crystal. I poured two fingers' worth and settled into one of the chairs with the score upon my lap, studying it as I brought the glass to my lips. The next instant I was spitting the wine back—it tasted like lamp oil. Frowning, I pushed it to the far side of the table and continued with my task, though after only a few moments of perusal I became intensely drowsy. I relented to my lethargy, set the pages aside and sat looking at the flames. They were a pale silvery orange and moved in a mechanical, almost hypnotic manner. I dozed then, and the dream came at once, as if it had been there only waiting for me to shut my eyes.

I saw my mother, the two-dimensional version of her from the amateur portrait above the mantel in my childhood home. She was doll-like and blunted in stature, the arms and legs and torso blocky. The face was too round, the skin a pasty and uniform peach, the sandy hair drawn back in a bright red ribbon—a style in which she had never worn in life. Her eyes were the only detail the artist had rendered with a modicum of accuracy: they were green, large, endearing. She stood in a long, low tunnel like the catacomb from my recurring nightmare, but here the walls were glass, and through them on either side was a press of compacted dirt and roots and coffin wood. My mother opened her heart-shaped lips and began to sing—a trifle she used to lull me to sleep with—though the voice was not hers but the viola's. The sound grew louder, splitting the casket boards. The walls shattered, disgorging a flood of grave-mool and bone and worm-tunneled flesh which covered her. And yet the song did not end; it altered pitch, became a wraith-like wail, and the voice was no longer the viola's, but that of my father, or rather, *his* wraith.

I awoke with a start, though my mind must have been still engaged in the dream, for in the fireplace I saw, for just an instant, a mash of distorted, moaning faces contained within the waggling flames. I squinted and leaned closer, but the harder I tried to see them, the more rapidly they faded, until finally they had vanished altogether as the fire resumed its slow and mesmerizing sway.

I had a sudden chill. Rain volleyed the orange glass of the lancet, thought it felt as though the dampness was somehow inside as well. I got up and put on my overcoat, loosening my cravat and removing the single key attached to a cord hanging around my neck before buttoning the coat to the top and raising the collar. Then I settled into the chair again and brought the oblong instrument case onto my lap, slid the key into the lock and raised the lid.

To look upon her, each time, is a gift. She lies in a form-fitted bed of crushed velvet. A crimson ribbon binds her neck. She is flat black under all light, and the grain lines of the yew tree from which she was carved are always visible, like familiar creases on an old hand. She is considered a long viola—17¾ inches—slender at the c-bouts, and curving voluptuously at the lower bouts. The pointed f-holes gape slightly and are pitched inward at a sharper angle than is standard, giving her a look of glaring. Small rounds of polished bone accentuate the outer fluting of her clenched fist scroll. She is flawless as the day she left her notorious maker's bench over two centuries ago. To touch her is the purest exhilaration; it prickles the fingertips, and numbs deep and anodyne when contact is prolonged. There is no greater soothing than the reverberation of her low C. How many illimitable hours have I spent alone, after the performances and the fêting, plucking, savoring that trance-inducing hum? I did this as I sat before the fire, murmuring that consoling note in unison in the hopes that it would aid the interminable minutes in passing.

At length I was summoned from my chamber by one of the servants and led downstairs and through the lower rear set of doors in the stair hall. The salle they opened into—the grossly understated and mundanely designated "great hall"—is certainly the grandest room in the castle, and the initial view, like all the others in this place, was stupefying. The hall was twice as long as the previous space, and though not as titanic in height, the figured hammerbeam roof stretching from end to end was no less spectacular. From the apex of this, set equidistant from one another, were three enormous chandeliers of elegantly figured wrought iron. Later I would count one hundred pillar-like tapers ringing each, all of them burning with that slow silken light which gave the dark wood the look of tarnished tin. Below these was a table with the capability of accommodating a king's soiree, beginning not far from the entrance and extending to the expansive red marble fireplace, so bright and veined with white striations that at first glance it resembled highly marbled meat.

    I saw the Count seated at the furthest end of the table, my father to his left and across from him a woman with a coiffed corona of curled lustrous red hair. To her right was a girl of perhaps fifteen. I heard my father regaling the trio with the story of my first recital at age nine for the eminent Lord Lionsbrüch, the much-embellished tale concluding as I approached the seat beside the old man. The three rose, the women curtsying as the Count introduced them as the Countess Marlena and their daughter, the lady Daeva. The latter regarded me with the gaze of a guileless ingénue—that unmitigated adoration which precludes introduction or conversation and has become, I must confess, increasingly irksome with time. Yet for all her naiveté, Daeva is a remarkably radiant being. Her large eyes sparkle like her father's, though they are more amber than iridescent yellow. Though wan and slightly greyish-green of flesh, she has small, pretty features; her ears are like intricately carved shells and her plush lips a lovely shade of muted rose. Her hair is a tangled bouffant of oddly interspersing white and blond tresses which rise off her head and trail down her back in long, snake-like blades. (There was something red-orange threaded through these at the ends ... were they petals? Leaves?)

    A servant—one of several I saw standing in the shadows of recessed alcoves along the walls—stepped forward and pulled out my chair for me. I was seated, and at once another of the sallow-visaged men filled my glass with scarlet wine. The Count raised his own, toasted our arrival with a lengthy prelude, and drained its contents with much relish and delight. My own, like the brandy in my chamber, was sour and corked; I glanced at my father, whose expression confirmed a similar flavor. I sought to spit it out but thought it impertinent, and so I swallowed the bitter stuff instead. This I regretted immediately; it burned like acid going down and boiled in the gut. Indeed, its effects have only just recently begun to diminish....

More servants came forward with silver dishes and began spooning an array of delicacies onto our plates. I was famished, having nothing in my stomach since the victuals at the roadside tavern, and that only temporarily, but the food was as foul and unpalatable as the wine. The Count and Countess nonetheless set about their meals with an almost indecent ravenousness. When queried with regards to our mutual lack of appetite, my father begged pardon and blamed dyspepsia, remarking that it is common after long voyages—a pretext to which I assented without hesitation.

The Countess asked, "What is the name of your new composition?" Looking at her then, I perceived that her eyes suffered from a convergence insufficiency and were, most curiously, different colors: one bright yellow similar to that of her husband, the other a dim emerald.

My father preëmpted my response: "He calls it 'The Three Tenets of Love.' It is a sonata in three parts."

"Oh? And what are these 'three tenets'?" asked the Count.

"Loyalty, Empathy, and Passion," I replied. These had been provisional titles; now that the piece is completed, I find the appellations exceedingly mawkish.

"And what of attraction?" Daeva said.

I looked from the Countess to her daughter, who was smiling at me, though in the next moment my gaze shifted again, this time to something startling in my periphery. I was staring into the lapidary amber eyes of a huge, stuffed white wolf standing on the mantel; hackles bristled, frozen forever in the moment before pouncing. Its lips were fixed into a snarl, its bared teeth the tinge of yellowed piano keys, its gums slick and wet. I swore that I could smell the thing—a musky, meaty stench just beneath the smoke from the burning logs. How had I not seen it previously? My mind was maddeningly blank as I attempted to recall whether or not it had been there when I entered the hall. It continues to baffle me as I write this.

Meanwhile, my father was saying to Daeva: "What you have mentioned is likely a *component* of Passion, my dear, but indeed a transient one."

"It seems to me the very essence of love," she replied.

"Perceived through the eyes of youth, perhaps," my father said with a patronizing smile. He chuckled and looked at the Count. "A beautiful and perceptive daughter you have, my lord."

"And inquisitive, alas," the Count said with a sigh, then raised his glass and downed his wine. His face seemed to be absorbing the color of it, and I surmised that his tippling must generally commence quite early. Daeva meanwhile appeared discomfited by her father's comment, as her own visage had flushed.

The Countess then asked if my father and I might offer a preview of the new work after dinner, to which the Count interjected: "My dear, these men have been traveling for days. Is it not discourteous to ask such of them?"

"My apologies," the Countess said, partly to her husband, partly to me. "I thought it was the gentleman's intention, seeing as that he has brought his viola along with him."

I said: "This instrument is an exceptionally rare and valuable family heirloom, my lady. It never leaves my sight."

"Yes," said the Count, "I understand that it is also a rather notorious instrument by the hand of a certain Cremortan luthier."

"The *Inamorta*," Daeva said. I locked eyes with the girl, and something clandestine seemed to pass between us, a shared understanding of sorts, though what this was I could not and still am not certain. Perhaps it was the sound of that name on her lips, one which, though known by all, is rarely spoken, as if it carries with it the potential of dark summoning.

"Is it true, Maestro?" the Count asked. "Is it indeed Giovanni Morturia's last creation?"

"It is no other," my father replied haughtily. The affirmation of this always gives him a great deal of pleasure, and me an equal measure of irritation.

"And what of the stories concerning the maker's wife?" said the Countess.

"Apocryphal tales, to be sure. The consequence of a long and misconstrued lineage," my father said.

"And what about its current master? What say you, Maestro Layne—has anything unusual occurred during the years of your stewardship?"

I had been looking at the wolf again—my attention given to an area near one of its lower incisors where a pool of spittle had gathered and was beginning to run over in a glistening line—when the Count addressed me. "Nothing to give them merit, sir," I said, with a forced smile. I believe I have become quite adroit in delivering the lie, flatly and with little reaction. Seeking to preserve my illusion of composure, I turned to the Countess and said: "With regard to your inquiry, my father and I would be pleased to play something for you this evening."

The old man winked at me as the Countess expressed her delight. To be sure, I had no desire to perform; on the contrary I was exhausted and wanted then only the oblivion of sleep. But Theodore, ever the politician, would only chastise me later had I not offered, and I have had my surfeit of 'duty before leisure' lectures. The Count, however, had somehow gleaned my true sentiments and suggested that we proceed to the music room so that my father and I might sooner find respite.

We rose and made our way through the great hall, my father flanked by the Count and the Countess, the latter taking him by the arm to assist him. Daeva slipped an arm through mine, asking if she might escort me. I acceded with reluctance and thanked her formally. A strong odor emanated from her—or perhaps her clothing?—an intriguing and to me unfamiliar *eau de parfum* concealing something acerbic and bitter beneath, like stale lilac or desiccated rose. Despite this, and despite her overt flaunting of girlish allure, she is surprisingly perspicacious and discerning, and most endearing of all, sympathetic. Her charm is emphasized by her proficiency in meaningful colloquy beyond the persiflage and banter which are regrettably de rigueur amongst the aristocracy. We spoke at length as we walked through the stair hall, pausing there to gaze up at the magnificent ceiling. The orbs there were pulsating slowly like fireflies in summer dusk, and the space was inexplicably redolent with the scents in accordance to that expired season: the attar of warmed flowers mingled with hints of wheat and the cooling of sun-baked thatch. She asked a torrent of questions about our "extravagant destinations," and about the famous and infamous who inhabit them. My detailing of these was met with the captivated awe of a captive girl, longing for the vicarious thrill of the adventures and anecdotes conveyed by a rare visitor. Naturally, she was considerably less interested in my disclosure of the dreary rigors of perpetual traveling and performing; even so, I took great pleasure in her company, joined intimately arm in arm as we strolled down the wing opposite the one that led to my father's quarters.

Ahead, the Count and Countess were leading my father toward the wall at the end of the corridor. It appeared to be a solid mirror and, just as I was pondering where exactly we were heading, the wall split into two outwardly opening panels, revealing a stylish concert hall, with exotic padauk paneling and boxes and seats of polished bronze. I am astonished by its acoustical properties, which are lacking in none of the five classical attributes—a feature especially impressive for a private theatre. The stage is small, with a fine piano and a small table for the placing of my instrument case. There are no footlights; rather, in keeping with the rest of the castle, that simultaneously murky and illuminate substance flows therein through long glass cylinders running tall to short like organ pipes on either side of the walls, descending in size as they near the orchestra section.

My father and I were left off by our hosts at a narrow stair leading to the stage. As we settled into our respective positions, they did the same in the three center seats of the front row, before the empty orchestra pit. I unpacked the viola and carried it to the footlights. I could feel the eyes on it. Typically this moment of beholding the scandalous object is accompanied by startled whispers, but the trio Canis made not a sound.

"Canzonetta in D minor," I said to the old man, who struck the first grave chords. I held the viola to my neck and felt it slide into place, that intimate, familiar *lock*—then the thread of black ice running through my fingertips and arm, to the core of my chest where it tingled in a cadence of needle taps. I raised the bow, brought it down, and as hair bit string a dark, sonorous moan filled the hall. The notes of the canzonetta unfurled in a guttural and wordless plea, an accentuation of grief so visceral I began involuntarily to weep. As previously mentioned, I was astounded by the room's aural qualities. The viola's martelé boomed like a cannon, its glissando glided with the fluidity of an unbridled stream, its pizzicato chirped like the call of a song-throated bird of prey. Though I perform invariably with my eyes closed, so potent and self-assured in that moment did I feel that I opened them to observe Daeva's reaction. She was indeed gazing raptly, not at me but the viola. One hand was balled in her lap, the other hovered loosely at the center of her chest. Inexplicably, by some trick of that mystifying light perhaps, I thought I saw something glowing beneath the latter hand, as if she were concealing an ember. Then, beyond her, I saw a man standing in the aisle near the entrance to the hall.

 He appeared somewhat out of focus, as if viewed from behind frosted glass, but I could nonetheless discern black hair and eyes of the same color stuck in a long and pallid face. His body was round and his ragged clothing too small; his black coattails stuck out like tail feathers and his white shirt was soiled and missing buttons. He wore a single adornment: a dull blue/black stone the size of a walnut stuck in a clasp and suspended by a leather cord. He was glaring at us with a look of such scorn that I, spooked as I was at his sudden appearance, would have had ended the piece prematurely had not the dark and relentless music been streaming through me at the speed of blood. And so the piece proceeded, errorless until the last note, which I drew out in a long and pulsating vibrato. It echoed briefly—like the crack of a pistol shot—and then all was silent again.

 No applause followed. (This is customary for those first hearing the viola.) The Countess was weeping, dabbing a handkerchief in the corners of her mismatched eyes, and the Count was gazing at me as if he'd had a profound revelation. I observed this in passing as I scanned the room for the man, who was nowhere to be found. I had the odd sensation that he had always been there, and had somehow been *revealed* by the music.

"Astonishing," said the Count. "The moaning of the wind ... the roar of the sea ... the cry of a brokenhearted maiden, the laughter of a child! It is life rendered into sound and nothing less."

Beside him the Countess suddenly wilted, a spell of faintness overwhelming her, and she fell forward into the arms of her husband and daughter. I descended the stairs with haste; by the time I reached them the lady was again conscious. Her color however remained poor, like greyed linen. The Count, looking much concerned, stated that he should like to get her to bed straightaway, and with profuse apologies and a fleeting goodnight the trio departed the hall.

I led my father down the stairs and out into the corridor, which had dimmed considerably and continued to darken as we made our way toward the stair hall. Our footsteps echoed flatly in the vastness, and that pleasing summer fragrance had altered with the light into a fug of mildew and damp. I attempted to increase the pace but it only brought on a spasm of coughing from the old man, who paused to down a dose from his pocket phial, and so I slowed again, my unease mounting as we ambled through the deepening shadows. I wanted to ask him if he'd seen the man in the grave-rotted clothes, but it seemed ill-timed to inquire about apparitions.

It was almost black by the time we reached the doors to the library. As we approached, my foot struck something that clattered, skittering down the stone floor. The eerie guards were gone—part of me was not disappointed in finding them so—and thus it took several minutes of fumbling for the knob. Upon entering, we were much relieved to find that the interior was not draped in a similar gloom. A slow dance of flames burned sweet smelling wood beyond the hearth, and the orbs glowed with a radiant shell-pink hue between the towering shelves of books, glittering the gilded titles on the spines. I started toward the bed, but the old man insisted that I first assist him in procuring a selection of volumes. I obliged him, retrieving those at which he aimed a gnarled finger, including a compendium of romantic verse, a classical treatise on musical pedagogy, a massive tome full of hand-colored maps, and a black and decrepit old tract with no title that was stuffed inharmoniously between two large and highly ornamented ones. I piled them on a table beside the bed and helped lower my father onto the mattress.

"Well, after all these years you've finally located it," I said as I settled into a chair beside the table with the stack of books. "Your personal paradise. You will no doubt petition the Count to keep us on indefinite retainer."

The old man grinned as he surveyed the room. "Extraordinary, is it not? Why, there must be *ten thousand* volumes within that case alone!" He picked up the first off the pile and turned it in his hands. Joy reduced his age by two decades or more. I lamented that what I was about to say would obliterate it.

"I dreamed of Mother today."

As anticipated, the look of content vanished, shadowed like a bloom-studded glen beneath the pall of brooding thunderheads. He set the book down and looked just past it at the twining coppery vine of the silken bedspread, tracing the pattern with his eyes.

"She resembled that picture above the fireplace in the old parlor. Do you remember the one of which I speak?"

"Yes," he said with a hint of impatience.

"She was singing. I had not thought about that, how she used to sing to me, since I was a child. The memory of her voice came to me upon waking, and it made me feel comforted in a way that I haven't felt in ... well, since that time, I suppose."

The old man said nothing, though his eyes had stopped traversing the woven curls. I was shuddering, my fingers tapping on the surface of the table. I made a fist, inhaled and exhaled a brisk breath and tried again.

"Do you ever dream of her?"

"That food was dreadful tonight, was it not?" he replied without looking up. "Positively *awful!* I hope for our sakes it isn't the standard fare of the region."

I closed my eyes, clenched my fist as tight as I could and then relaxed it; the nail impressions remaining in my palm. I asked measuredly: "Would you like me to fetch you something from the dry stores in your trunk?"

"Thank you, but I am not hungry, only tired." He looked up at me then with the smile of the proud father on his lips, the one he wears at the courts of princes and queens and dauphins and contessas, the same one those latter royals wear when they look upon their lapdogs.

I rose from the chair. "I will say goodnight to you then."

"Goodnight, my son."

As I departed I stole a glance at him through the gap in the door. He was not in fact reclining and shutting his eyes, but putting on his glasses and opening the cover of the book on his lap.

I stepped out into the dark and closed the door. The corridor was no longer dark; it seemed I blinked, and the globes were again lustrous, the fresh scent restored, and the guards returned to their post. Alarmed by their sudden reappearance I cried out, felt at once foolish and made apologies, but the stolid pair with their rigid faces and narrowed, dull eyes (did I indeed see their eyes? I cannot now precisely recall...) gave no reply to my utterances, nor any indication of being in the least aware of my presence.

I started toward my room, not altogether at ease leaving my father with those uncanny sentinels just beyond his door. But then they were at nearly every door, weren't they?—and moving swiftly and with perfunctory grace to open each one as I approached. Entering my chamber, I decided that my apprehension was irrational. Engaging me in conversation was not, after all, a component of their duty.

Unlike Father, I *was* hungry. From my trunk I gathered and assembled an impromptu and rather crude meal of dried fruit, buckwheat cakes, cured beef, and bitter chocolate. I also retrieved from my stores a split of claret, which I uncorked and downed in gulps between mouthfuls of the leathery fare. At length, with my hunger sated and the warmth of the wine blooming in my chest, I took the viola from its case, sank into the chair before the fire, and holding it guitar-style, plucked out the tune my mother had sung in the dream. I had closed my eyes, reposing in the hum of the pizzicato, when beneath it came a soft rapping on the door.

I set the viola in its case and crossed the room. As I was nearing the doors, they suddenly opened, and Daeva stepped inside, just enough for them to close behind her. She had changed dresses; now she wore a simple layered white gown, gossamer and slightly yellowing along the seams. Beneath the gauzy silk and cotton I spied an elaborate and web-like necklace of strands the shade and luster of pewter. These rose up and over her collarbones and wound around her throat like a garrote. At the center of it was a large jewel of the same dark shade and size as a horse's eye. She said nothing, remaining those several paces away while regarding me as if I were some gallery piece for which she had a marked affinity. So unnerving was this silence that I felt compelled to speak; she, however, preëmpted me by coming forward and placing something in my hands.

"For you," she said.

I looked down and saw cupped in my palms a small viola carved from porcelain or ivory, or perhaps some form of bone. As I look upon it now, lying on the table before me, I am unable to make the distinction. I stared at the object in utter bewilderment. This was not a miniature representation of any viola—it was *the* Inamorta, replicated to the finest detail: the clenched-hand scroll, the erratic grain lines, the brooding f-holes. Even my initials were carved in the tiniest letters on the treble-side foot of the bridge, just as they were on the wooden one on the real instrument. It has strings as well, impossibly thin filaments which hover over the fingerboard and wind in perfect coils around the pegs. When I graze my thumb over them they resonate with a faint chime.

When I asked where she had gotten it, she replied with something even more astounding.

"I made it."

"*You* did?" I said, incredulous. "But how?"

She went to the fireplace, where the real Inamorta lay in its open case. "Such fragile beauty," she said softly. "All that power contained in such a delicate form, dependent upon you for preservation. What a burden it must be."

I answered that, on the contrary, I considered it the greatest of privileges. She did not respond; she was staring down intently at the instrument as if it were a corpse in a coffin. I took a quiet step toward her and asked if she had enjoyed the music this evening. She looked up at me and said: "Of course. Did you think that I wouldn't?"

"One can never be certain," I said, embarrassed that she had exposed my seeking for a compliment.

"You are of the *virtuosi*," she said. "I'm sure you never fail to please."

I opened my mouth to reply, then closed it again.

"May I touch it?"

"I beg your pardon?"

"The Inamorta," she said. Again, that name spoken aloud. Such liberty she took with it! She raised a hand and hovered it palm-down above the viola, as if warming it over an open flame. In three strides I closed the distance and shut the case. She drew back, uttering a startled cry.

"Forgive me. That was rather presumptuous," she said.

"No, please ... do not apologize," I said, feeling suddenly unpardonably rude. "I am unaccustomed to anyone touching it save for myself."

"I suppose that makes you a worthy steward indeed," she said. Her eyes lingered on the closed case another instant or two. "I should leave you to yourself now."

"I hope you do not find me discourteous," I called after her as she crossed the room. When she reached the door she turned back.

"Will you walk with me to-morrow? I would like to show you the garden. It is sublime, even at this time of year."

I told her that I must rehearse in the morning. And the afternoon? she inquired. I asked how to get there; she said that she would come for me. When she had gone, I locked the door and the instrument case and sat again in front of the fire. The flames were fading—and I along with them. I undressed and got into bed. It is quite plush and snug, but sleep, alas, would not come. For a restive hour I lay there, pondering the events of this unsettling day, until an image coalesced in my mind as if spun from the shadows.

I saw the wolf upon that scarlet mantel in the great hall, its eyes luminescent in the dark. It stepped onto the table where it paused to sniff the rancid food and my chair before moving off through the hall.

This was the image which got me out of bed and to this desk, where I am in the hopes that expelling it onto the page will aid in dismissing these wild thoughts and afford me at last some semblance of rest....

Evening, 17th November, 1799
Teethsgate, my father's chamber

I write this—a few words while my father sleeps between rehearsals—to document to-day's strange occurrences. Our dinner, delivered by a pair of those grey-faced servants who move in such languid eeriness and with such reptilian slowness, sits uneaten on silver trays. The beef with capers and burgundy sauce, fluted potatoes, truffles, galantine of hen, and strawberry tart are all delectable in appearance, yet flavorless and inedible as bark, and the smell is markedly offensive, though I would rather suffer this than have the servants return to retrieve it. The old man and I assuaged our appetites with an uninspiring repast of rye bread slathered with marmalade, and two tumblers apiece of ale obtained from the squalid tavern where I ate my last substantial meal. What is one to think? This is only the most recent of the many disquieting mysteries which, I am finding, abound in this place.

Consider my walk with Daeva earlier in the castle's garden. I was made to go in search for it when, as the afternoon waned, she did not come for me as she said she would. After a bewildering ramble through this leviathan of stone and mirror searching for an exit, I happened upon a set of doors in the stair hall that I had not noticed during my second and even third time wandering there. They opened onto a long and rectangular courtyard enclosed by high walls of undressed ashlar which were covered, almost wooly with, tawny leaves the shape of elongated hearts. Here again was that unusual perfume I had earlier smelled on Daeva; then it had been a pleasant accent, but here, surrounded by it, I found it nauseatingly cloying. Flagstone paths led along the perimeter and diagonally between beds of orange pincushion flowers and sunburst ranunculus. The latter walkways were pointed inward toward the courtyard's center, where stood a fountain with a huge granite wolf rearing on its hind legs like a royal lion. Water gushed from its every orifice, coursing perpetually down its hideously vulpine rictus and black-slimed body. The statue is repugnant in both form and implication, for beneath one of its enormous paws I saw, lying prone, a stone man. The claws were sunk into his back and the water burbled, as if in imitation of blood from his wounds.

There was a sound overhead like boulders rolling through the tombstone-grey clouds. Instrument case in hand, I started down a random path, scanning the garden for Daeva, but found her nowhere. Then, at the back of the courtyard I saw her emerge through a gated doorway set in the rear wall, which appeared to open into a tumulus swelling on the outside of that same wall. She was apparition-like, wearing a trailing and diaphanous white gown, clearly antique and perhaps modified; I have no reference for either the style or the period from which it originates. Her hair was raked into a white-yellow nimbus around her face. As she came near, I saw she was cradling a limp white crow in her arms. Its neck had been wrenched or violently twisted; blood ran from its pink eyes, staining its cottony feathers. When I inquired as to what had happened to the unfortunate creature, Daeva blandly replied that it "had died," with no further explication. I said that it was most lamentable, as the bird appeared to be of a rare breed and beauty.

"They're a nuisance, actually," she said. "They steal the Lovers' Tongues for their nests. And they shit on the flagstones."

I was shocked by her indelicate use of profanity; and doubly so when she crossed to the fountain, pitched the bird indifferently into the pool and rinsed her hands under the jet of water streaming from the wolf's penis. She wiped her palms on the hems of her dress, and in the next moment was taking my arm and guiding me down one of the pathways. She asked if I was comfortable in my "modest" chamber. I remarked that it was hardly that.

"Even compared to the many royal apartments in which you have slept?" she said.

"Quite superior to, in fact," I said, which seemed to please her much.

"And what about your father? I understand that he is ill."

"He is gouty and has recently been afflicted with croup; conditions made worse by our journeyman lives."

"Did you show him what I made for you?"

"I did, though ..." I paused, seeking the right words. "There was an accident."

During the morning's rehearsal I had indeed shown Daeva's remarkable creation to my father, who was as befuddled as I in attempting to explain how the girl had fashioned it. He suggested that perhaps somewhere amidst the stacks she had discovered a rendering of it by an artist of an earlier generation, a notion which I dismissed, citing the absence of my initials in any of those prospective pictures. I told Daeva that I had clumsily knocked it off a table with my bow, but the truth was the little facsimile had exploded while my father and I were performing the third movement of the new composition. As we reached the conclusion of the Passion, the viola grew louder, reaching a volume I had never heard it attain. On the final note there was a shattering sound. I felt something small and sharp strike my cheek, drawing blood. When I opened my eyes I saw a tiny white fist at my feet. I picked up the scroll and held it aloft for my father to see. He was carefully collecting shards from the top of the piano. Hovering in the air was a fine puff of dust—hanging in the silence as we stared perplexed at one another, before settling upon the flame-orange rugs.

"Terribly careless of me," I reiterated. I supposed her to be crestfallen by this confession, but her eyes, the shade of gold in shadow, regarded it contemplatively for a few moments and then looked away. "Do not fret. As I said, it was only a trinket."

"I've been pondering how you managed to duplicate it with such accuracy. It must have taken you ages."

"I have a considerable amount of time to myself," Daeva said, disregarding the initial part of my statement. "It is good to have your company, *maestro*."

"Do not call me that, I beg you," I sighed.

"Why not?"

"Because it supplants my name and sets me apart."

"Nevertheless, it is who you are."

"Nevertheless, I despise it."

A gust of wind swept along the courtyard walls, rustling the ivy and wafting flourishes of the sickly scent toward us. And there once more beneath it was that sharp and bitter smell, like dog, or was it dog urine? I glanced back at the statue, which of course had not moved, and then at Daeva and sniffed.

"All right then, *Jonas*. What of your family? Is it only you and your father?"

"For more than a decade now. My mother died when I was nine."

"Did you see it happen?"

At this I hesitated, once again taken aback by her insouciance. "I saw the beginning of the end. She was choking on her own blood. My father shut me out of the room until it was over. We buried her a few days later; the house and our things were sold, and we were on the road within the month."

"Do you ever wish that you could stop?"

"Sometimes I wish that we could go home, though of course there is no 'home', as it were, in which to return. What I long for most will to you seem prosaic...."

She looked at me curiously.

"... my own bed," I said.

Daeva's arm tightened around mine. We had reached the gate at the center of the wall, and I paused there to look through the bars at the stone door set behind them. It was ancient and there was something carved on the surface in low relief—an emblem or an escutcheon. Though it was in shadow, I was able to perceive a wing and the head of a large bird of prey. Beneath the intensifying perfume of the heart-shaped leaves I smelled emanating from it a stench of decay.

"What is this?" I asked.

"The entrance to the crypt," Daeva whispered. "All of my forbearers lie below, as will mother and father one day. We are the last, you see."

I turned to her. "And what of the man at last night's performance? Is he not some relative?"

"Man?" she said. Her voice had not altered, but I swore I felt her stiffen beside him.

"I saw a man dressed in black and rather ill-fitting clothing. He was watching us from the aisle just off from where you sat with the Count and Countess."

"I know no one of that description. It is only us three, and the servants. Perhaps you mistook one of them?"

"It is possible, yes," I said, frowning.

"Come, I want to give you something," Daeva said suddenly, pulling me away from the gate and hurrying me toward an ivy-clad alcove in one of the perimeter walls. There, she plucked a score of the leaves and began weaving them tip to stem in a ring. The resident wasps drifted in alarm from her as if she were exuding smoke. With her back turned, I observed her with uninhibited scrutiny. Her dress was more brittle and discolored than I had initially perceived. There was what looked like a faint water stain running from the left shoulder down to her waistline, and the fabric crinkled and crackled like crumpling paper as she grasped at the leaves. There was no sheen to her hair; it was more like an old wig long bereft of a comb. Her movements were stiff and slow, and it seemed to me as though I was watching not a girl but a life-sized doll in motion. In the shadowy alcove, her flesh was the color of cloudy water, though with a translucent quality which stratified her features. Grey veins twisted along the surface like river snakes, and beneath them, like something surfacing, I could see the vague outline of jaw and orbital socket, as if her skull were black. Looking at her, I wondered if she might be ill; gravely, perhaps.

But as she returned to the path, her task complete, this unwell impression seemed to diminish entirely. She bade me to lower my head, then hung the knotted strand of leaves around my neck.

"A gift," she said.

"But you've already given me one," I replied.

"This one will not break so easily, unless you choose to," she said. I lifted it off my chest, gazing at the little hearts. She came forward and took my hands, pressing herself against me. "You are a rare creature, Jonas. Handsome and pure and … *powerful*. I should like to know all of your secrets … all those you have denied others … all those *forbidden* ones.…"

I opened my mouth to reply, and suddenly her lips were there—tender, soft, and yielding as I returned the kiss—and then it was over, and I was watching her run off and disappear into the through a door in one of the castle turrets. I stared at them as rain began spotting the flagstones, then opened my hand and looked at the leaves lying on my palm which curled up along the edges from my body heat.

I followed after her, hastening up the path as the deluge began in earnest, and pulled open the turret door. A stone stairway wound high and tight up the column. I started up them, propelled by the perfume of the Lovers' Tongues and that transitory moment of Daeva's lips on mine. She would be waiting for me at the top, I knew it. *Duty first,* said my father's voice in my head—those words he had embedded in my brain during the earliest days of my musical training with the same import as scales and modes. *Duty first* when I begged him as a youth that we might return home, quitting this peripatetic existence, *duty first* whispered with caution every time a young courtière looked upon me with eyes like open doors that would permit me anywhere within. Two words, these, which triggered guilt and exasperation and unmerited shame. I had long gnawed at their bindings, and as I hurried up the tower I felt them at last loosen and fall away.

But my moment of emancipation was eclipsed by the confounding emptiness of the small cylindrical chamber. Nonplussed, I stood staring at the rain streaking past the arrow-slit portals, then circled the space but discovered no means of ingress or egress. Had I missed some other way on my frenetic ascension?

I started down again, step by slow step this time, but saw no doorway. Upon reaching the bottom, I was doubly startled to find that the door *there* had vanished.

What was going on?

Frantically and rather futilely I pressed against the stone, but found it was no illusion. I thought perhaps I could call for help through one of the narrow windows at the top of the turret and again wound my way up the column. This time, however, there was a landing about halfway up, and a door—yes, suddenly a *door*—standing open, and beyond, the corridor which led to my room....

I will pause here, as the old man stirs and is in need of some water—

18th November, 18–
Teethsgate, my chamber

Last night I had the dream again. Or, perhaps, I should call it a cousin of that recurring night-terror, as the mood was the same, though the events were not. I was not this time being pursued by some mongrel abomination, but viewing from some omniscient vantage, observing the wolf that stands upon the mantel of the great hall of this castle. It was circling and sniffing the base of a massive and ancient tree whose entire aspect was of acute desiccation and decay, as if its roots had tapped some poisoned cistern. Its trunk resembled a hank of wet and twisted brown hair, and its fruitless branches ramified from that mummified core like sun-baked snakes. Oddly, I could feel the deadwood, as if it and my own flesh were one. My limbs were dry and aching, and the wolf's urine was hot and bitter-smelling when it sprayed the bark. It paused, nose to the soil, and then began to dig, uncovering at length a small oblong box. I heard my heart knocking inside, thumping against the lid. The wolf reached out to open it, and its hand had human fingers, and as these unfastened the clasps the wolf turned and grinned at me, its eyes silver mirrors.

I woke, and in that moment I *smelled* the thing in my room. I sat up in the colossal bed, my head feeling as if after a night of too much claret, and scanned the dimness. I saw no wolf, but noticed that the door was opened slightly. I rose and crossed to it, my heart still knocking as if against that wooden lid, and stuck my head through the gap. There stood the guards, stoic and statuesque. I asked if anyone had entered my room but got no response, and my further inquiries in this regard resulted in the same silence, as if I were speaking to stone. I closed the door, bolted it, and turned back to the room where I found the globes alight, and flames rising in the fireplace without any apparent origin of ignition....

Disconcerted, I dressed at once and went down to my father's chamber. I decided not to tell him about the dream or the incident in the tower, for he was in a similar state of unease, complaining of, amongst other things, a persistent scratching noise coming from behind the arch against which his bed was pushed. I moved the latter away and saw that there was a door there, quite unlike the others in the castle. It was scored with age and there was an iron ring at the center, which I pulled and then pushed, but in either direction found it absolutely unyielding.

"Might it have been mice?" I asked.

"Not likely," the old man replied. "At any rate, it was not the primary dilemma that kept me awake." He produced the little brown bottle from his pocket and shook the few remaining drops therein. "I am rationing it."

I told him that that would not do, and that I would go into town myself to procure more for him. Surely there was an apothecary, and besides, we needed our own provisions, seeing as the food here was not only unpalatable, but most likely indigestible. Together we looked at the guéridon trolley, its three tiers lined with inedible haute cuisine.

"Yes ... we shall indeed," he said.

"Have you anything left in your trunk?" I asked.

"Some figs ... a bit of smoked ham, I think," he said drearily.

I gathered these (a paltry amount indeed, alas) and we ate our provender quietly and with little enthusiasm. My eyes kept returning to that arched doorway over the old man's bed. There was something about it that epitomized the fantastical elements of the castle ... or, better said, contradicted them, for it seemed that if it could be budged it would open upon the truth of this place. I am not certain why I felt this, or what this intuited veiled reality is precisely, but the sense that something is lurking behind the façade of the castle has increased the longer we are here.

After our pitiful refection, I asked my father if he was well enough for the day's rehearsal. His reply was most Theodore-like: "No, but that has little to do with it," he grumbled. Then he began to cough—a frightfully deep and clotted sound accompanied by a discharge of much red mucus. He downed the rest of the bitter green potion, then sent me again to his trunk, this time for a vessel of Madeira, which I procured though I knew that it would only exacerbate his gout. He drank until his chest seemed to settle and his hands steadied. I insisted that he rest, but he would have none of it, demanding that I assist him to the piano. Once in place upon his bench, he wrapped his smeary round glasses around his ears and, with a slight lift of the head, scowled at the manuscript for a second at the "Empathy" movement I put before him.

"You've changed the tempo."

I conceded that I had.

"Do you think it's necessary, beginning in *presto*? Don't you think it a bit *boastful*?"

"'It's what the music calls for,'" I replied. This had been his response every time I grumbled as a child about a piece being too difficult. *It's what the music wants, what it calls for, and therefore must be done.* Once I had acquired the Inamorta, this maxim became redundant, and went the way of my first viola, put away and forgotten.

"We shall see about that," he said, and, glowering, he began without me.

The piece *was* much improved at a more rapid tempo (we concurred by not speaking of it further). Indeed, he spoke little to me during the rehearsal, and I caught him glaring once or twice at the viola. When the music was over, he at once took to his bed again, stating tersely that he would like to sleep some before supper and, turning toward the wall, said nothing further.

I returned to my room for my overcoat and leather satchel and, with the latter over my shoulder and the instrument case in hand, departed the castle. Rather than take the road which ran too closely and precipitously along the sheer land's end, I skirted the southern aspect of the keep and traversed the mile or so to town following the meandering border of the forest where the grade of the terrain was more gradual. It was brisk, and the brooding pall of fog had not dissipated; rather, shifted, hovering now in the tree tops. Ah, what a rarity indeed though were these sparse moments—that time which is my *own*. Despite the threat of inclement weather, I took much delight in the invigorating downhill trek. The cool air was a balm in my lungs, and in my exhilaration I reached Larmes Harbor in less than an hour.

My happiness was tempered by the bleak town square, which was still and hushed as if abandoned. I knew of course that it was not, which made the silence all the more disquieting. As I walked along that single desolate thoroughfare I could feel myself being watched from behind a corner of a curtain here, a peephole in a door there. Instinctively I gripped the handle of the instrument case tighter, and lowered my head so that my face was mostly concealed behind the raised collar of my overcoat. In retrospect, I suppose this behavior was tactless and did little to alleviate the trepidations of an apprehensive populace. I knew not what they feared, though what I saw next affirmed that there was indeed ample cause for collective suspicion.

I came upon the wall of a defunct counting house, where upon had been pasted several broadsides, each with a rendering of a face, and above each of these the same grim word in block capitals: MISSING. There were ladies and elderly men and roustabouts and merchants. Below each cursory sketch was a brief block of text describing the individual, and detailing the last place they were seen. There were in total perhaps forty of these notices, spanning from several months previous up to the present week. The earliest were faded and brittle, and there were empty spaces between them where some of the older ones had come detached and blown away. As I was studying these, a young girl, her apron cradling a hoard of vegetables and glass bottles, rounded the corner and clinked up the alley toward me. She walked quickly; her eyes fixed on the ground ahead of her and thus she did not notice me until I began to speak, inquiring if there was an apothecary in Larmes Harbor. Her terror at finding me there—unknown, and before that wall—must have been extreme, for she shrieked as if I were death itself beckoning her, and fled past me down one of the narrow passages off the alley.

    I proceeded along the main road, peering through the cloudy windows of the closed businesses and public buildings—a chandler's, a tailor's, a solicitor's, et cetera—with a rapidly intensifying sense of dread. It occurred to me that whatever had caused this village-wide confinement was still transpiring, and I became in that moment nervously aware of my overt presence in the deserted square. Then, at the juncture where the road split—curving left and continuing along the waterfront—I spied what appeared to be the town's general provisions store. Like the other façades, it was dark, but here the door was ajar, forced open apparently. I advanced with prudence, mounting the stoop and hesitating at the top stair whereupon I paused to listen. Nothing stirred within. I would in no other case have entered—trespassing as it were, and on the scene of a potential burglary no less—but my desperation, for my father's sake, as well as my need to be off the road, impelled me over the threshold and inside.

    The interior had indeed been ransacked. This was observable not only by the many empty shelves and barrels but the shattered jars and spilled baskets lying on the floor. The townsfolk, it seemed, were pilfering the wares herein unimpeded, a notion which hinted darkly of the fate of the shop's proprietor. I picked my way through the aisles gathering what I found that remained: four turnips, a broken parsnip, a package of barley, three tins of salted pork, and a loaf of bread recovered from beneath an upturned chair. At the rear of the store was a carved wooden counter, and behind this, lined in small square recesses along the wall, was a pharmacopoeia of powders, serums, balms, tonics, and potions. Though many had been snatched, I recognized amongst those which remained the familiar brown flask containing that malodorous moss-green tincture. I stuffed this in my shoulder sack along with the other goods and, before I left, took a few gold coins from my pocket and left them beneath the counter; a gesture, if nothing else, of auspicious optimism for the absent purveyor.

Emerging onto the street, I immediately started back in the direction of Teethsgate. As I approached the alley where I had previously stood regarding the Missing notices, I was startled by the sudden appearance of the same young girl who had earlier run off at the sight of me. Now accompanied by several other children of varying ages, she came forward, rather boldly, looked down at the instrument case and then up at me again. She asked if I were a musician, to which I replied yes, I was. One of the boys wanted to know where I was from. I told him that I had come down from the castle. This response educed unanticipated alarm; several of the children fled as if I were some long-rumored monster which had at last shambled down from the great pile on the mountain into their town. The few that remained, a pair of twin boys and the young girl, wanted to know: Would I play them something? I told them that my father was ill and I must bring him medicine without delay. This they did not gauge with any apparent comprehension of gravity or promptitude.

"But you already have your violin with you," one of the boys said. He had a lazy eye and was incessantly scratching his louse-ridden scalp. I corrected him on the type of instrument.

"May we see it?" the girl asked.

"It is very valuable, and susceptible to humidity I'm afraid," I said, eyeing the road ahead. The sack was becoming heavy, and I had awaiting me a long and uphill trek back to the castle.

"Come, we're too common and sullied for *his* kind," his twin said with the bitter dejection of one accustomed to disappointment. Though I wanted nothing more than to depart the dismal Larmes Harbor, I felt the bag of supplies sliding off my shoulder. I knelt and laid the oblong box upon the cobbles like a common street busker. "Perhaps I have time for one short piece...."

The three children erupted in acclamation as I unpacked the viola, though at the sight of its bitumen visage they fell at once silent. I removed the bow, twisted the button, made a couple of passes of the cake of rosin over the hair. I plucked the strings from low to high—CGDA: in tune, it was *always* in tune.

The music was like a siren in the silent town square. I saw faces appear at windows and around half-opened doors of buildings I had previously supposed vacant. Near the middle of the piece I glimpsed a woman passing through the center of the square. She stopped several yards off from the children, not to listen to the music but ostensibly to scowl at me before continuing on, head down, her arms hugging a grey worsted shawl around her narrow frame as she slipped down a side street.

I stared in that direction for several seconds after she'd gone and the music had ended, while the children applauded and cried out *Again!* Her expression had perturbed me deeply, for in it I saw an offense more reprehensible than the haughty indiscretion of performing for an audience of juveniles, who should by all accounts be huddled in their homes, safe from whatever lurked ghoul-like in their midst. Her glare suggested that she had intimated from the viola something repulsive, vulgar even, which had in turn induced revulsion, not only for the music but for *me*.

I could not cease thinking about her as I started back, feeling very much a pariah, and ready to return to the castle, despite my increasing apprehension of the place. The children followed me to the edge of the village. I glanced back when I was several yards up the incline, expecting to see one close behind me like a patted stray cat presuming to have found its new owner. None had followed, and the townsfolk had shut themselves back in their houses. The show was over, and Larmes Harbor was again silent as a plague town.

I encountered the fog about midway up the hillside. It materialized suddenly; I had sensed no palpable shift in temperature, nor had I observed the mist of an approaching storm moving inland. The thickening shroud grew denser, occluding not only sight but sound. The rasping ebb and flow of the tide faded gradually, and then entirely, until there remained only my own distressed inhalations and exhalations. I increased my pace, though my legs were already burning from the climb; in my panic I must have drifted sharply left, for the sound of my feet upon the loose stones of the cliff road stunned me to a halt. How near had I been to plummeting off? Five feet? Two? In the next moment, this terror was eclipsed by another when, quite near to me, I heard a low growl, followed by footsteps on the path, and then, emerging from the white, I saw hovering waist-high to me two pale lights, like candle flames through frosted glass. No living eyes burned as such, and in my mind I began to catalog the all manner of mythical beasts said to haunt these locales: gytrash, shagfoal, barghest. They grew brighter as the thing came closer, and in a reaction born of terror, I clasped the instrument case to my chest and ran in the direction of the forest.

It pursued, with such speed that it should have at once overtaken me. It seemed, however, to be playing a game; coming close, then darting away, prancing in, then scampering back. Suddenly on my left I felt it strike. My coat tore as the thing held, jerked—then released and bounded off. It struck again, this time gashing the shoulder sack. I heard several of the items therein topple onto the grass. My god, the smell of the thing! The reek of its ensanguined maw spurred me faster through the blankness, clinging to the oblong case as I awaited the next blow. Then, as if cast from a reverse torch, a channel of darkness spanned before me, parting the fog and disclosing a rain-streaked view of the bald land and the forest and, at the periphery of the scene, Teethsgate. I ran toward the vision, certain to be brought down before I arrived there. When at last I stepped forth from the shadow-lined tunnel and was returned, as it were, to sight and sound, I looked back and found that both my pursuer and the fog vanished, as if neither had been there at all.

By the time I reached the castle I was soaked through and shivering. Mounting the stairs and reaching the door, I was shocked when met there not by one of the stone-faced servants, but the Countess herself. She was aghast at finding me in such a state—drenched and disheveled—and asked why I had ventured out in such conditions.

"My father was out of his medication," I said as I stood dripping on the mirrored floor of the foyer.

She glanced at the bulking bag hanging on my shoulder. "I see," she said. "Surely you did not have to go yourself. We have footmen who can be dispatched for such necessities."

"I did not want to trouble anyone," I said, attempting a smile.

The Countess glanced at the guards flanking the door behind us and then back at me, her mismatched eyes blazing in the smoldering sconce light. She drew near, gripped my arm and whispered in a voice that was both thin and sharp: "There are rumors of evil and abduction in the village; a man in black that stalks his prey indiscriminate of rank or title. You are too vital to be snatched from us by such a random monster. I implore you, *maestro*, do not venture there again, for any reason...."

Startled, I nodded vigorously in assent, and she released me. As she did, I noticed the room brighten once more, and along with it, the Countess's wall-eyed gaze dim to that of dulled marbles.

"Now, we shan't risk you catching a chill. I have ordered a bath drawn. The servants will show you to the *salle de bains*." She gestured to one of the men, who came forth at once and bade me follow him through a panel that had opened in the wall on my left, adjacent to that which led to the stair hall.

We passed through a low stone passage lit warmly by flames rising from crescent-shaped protrusions from the walls. They burned freely, though what they were burning I could only conjecture, for there was no scent of oil or other fuel present in the air around us. The servant proceeded slowly, at a grave pace, and as I followed him I found myself scrutinizing his appearance. He was rather unkempt and scruffy, his coattails and breeches streaked dark red. One of his sleeves was torn, and the hair on the back of his head stuck up on one side like the feathers of a shot pheasant. I could not escape the singularly disquieting notion that these in sum suggested that he had been at some point *dragged*.

At the end of the corridor was an arched doorway; the hinge screech was piercing in the narrow hall. I saw a semi-circular room beyond glowing like late summer light. Its tangible warmth drew me nearer. The servant stood in profile beside the entrance waiting for me to pass through. There was something so discomposingly familiar about him (though *what* was not immediately evident) that my curiosity—or was it my instinct for self-preservation?—demanded an answer. It was his stillness and, despite his task, seeming ignorance of my presence which prompted my brazen pausing upon the threshold to scrutinize him. He made no objection of my audaciousness, only waited, automaton-like, until I had moved within the room after which he without hesitation closed the door.

This incident, like the encounter with the woman in the town square, continued to trouble me even as I began to take in the splendor of the *salle de bains*. It was a mere nook compared to the castle's other apartments, and yet the subtle grandiosity of the vaulted ceiling, pale pearlescent walls, and porcelain and marble appointments were in keeping with the overall design. At the center of the room was a long white tub with tall sides and on one end a round and graceful projecting lip. Curls of steam rose from it slowly, almost hypnotically, dissipating as they drifted upward toward the arched apex. Above the tub, hanging from a glimmering silver cord, was an enormous version of those enigmatic glowing glass orbs, stewing with that smoky coral light. There was a tall frameless mirror with beveled edges standing unsupported at a slight angle (set into the floor?) at the center of the curving rear wall, and beside it a table on which I saw a dry suit of my own clothing, impeccably folded and laid out, and next to this, a towel topped with a single Lover's Tongue leaf.

Piqued as I was at finding my things there, plucked from my chamber—my trunk, no less—without permission, the care with which everything had been arranged abated my outrage. My sopping clothing by this point had begun to assume the warmth of the room and felt uncomfortably tepid and spongy. I placed the instrument case and the bag of goods beside the mirror and began to undress, shedding the sodden garments piece by piece. The sultry atmosphere instantly surrounded me, a sensation most pleasant. Even the stone beneath my bare feet was warm. As I turned to enter the bath, I caught sight of myself in the mirror and halted. The glass was cloudy from the steam, and the angle at which the mirror had been propped rendered the likeness somewhat distorted. But neither of these accounted for the hallucination which I was doubtless seeing.

True, it was indeed Jonas Layne: there was the oval visage with the deep-set blue eyes; the bracket-like collarbones; the narrow torso; the pale thatches of hair and the slightly bulbous knees. And yet—certain idiosyncrasies which had been part of me since birth were inexplicably vanished. I appeared altered, like a re-worked painting. My skin no longer had a sallow pallor; it was now sleek and golden, a slim barrier contouring the refined muscles of my arms and torso. I ran my fingers along the defined abdominals, cupped my genitals which were bulky and weighty like ripe fruit drooping a branch. I was lean, hard, flawless—the ideal male image, a model for all those casts in bronze and sculptures in marble.

And yet ... where was the birthmark near my navel? Why did my eyes gleam in that frighteningly pellucid way, like polished cobalt baubles? What had happened to the dark crescents beneath them, and what of the graying teeth? Most disconcertingly of all, where was the large maroon patch, like blood-soaked cloth, stretching from my left shoulder to chin, the scar from the viola's cold burn? No, the form before me was not *the* Jonas, it was the *ideal* Jonas, stripped of the strain and wear. I wanted to turn away, but I did not—then I did not want to turn away, but I did, ultimately too unsettled by the figment to consider it any longer.

I stepped into the bath; the water was the ideal temperature and slid luxuriously over my limbs. It seemed to pull me in, and I surrendered thus, sinking into the balmy pool until submerged to my neck. Though the surface stilled, beneath it the water continued to stir, a current coursing over me like a hundred caressing hands. I became almost narcotically sedate, drew a long shuddering breath, held it, and slipped my head under.

How shall I write this without it sounding mad? Submerged in that soothing elixir, I heard voices; they were distant, as if I were standing outside a closed and crowded room. The faint cacophony spanned the entire human emotive range: speaking, singing, laughing, crying, screaming. I lay there listening as if under a spell, bubbles rising from my nose and mouth, arms weightless in the water, hair swaying like sea grass. I opened my eyes at length, certain I would see them. I did indeed see a face; it was not one of the nameless clamoring multitude, but Daeva, kneeling beside the tub and looking down at me.

I rose up in a shot, swallowing a gulp of water in my haste and choking on it. Daeva continued to regard me, without moving from where she knelt. She was wearing what appeared to be a loose collection of bands of linen of multifarious shades of white and pink, which wound around her upper form as if a partially wrapped mummy and appeared, it must be said, as though they might be unwrapped by merely pulling a single one of the dangling strips. I drew my knees up to my chest and said: "What do you want?" I hadn't meant for it to sound so brusque, and Daeva's reaction was indeed one of surprise.

"I heard you went to the village." I admitted that I had. "Why?" she asked.

"Is it requisite that I provide an explanation?"

Piqued, she turned away from me and faced the mirror. "I only wanted to make certain you were all right. There are dark rumors of something stalking the village...." She turned sharply then and said: "Did you speak to anyone?"

I said that I hadn't. She knew that I was lying, but what of it? I was myself piqued by the liberty she had taken in obtruding unannounced upon me here, though I could not deny the simultaneous salacious thrill of her presence. I wondered: How long had she been standing there? And then with heart-lurching panic I remembered the instrument case.

I sat up straight and cocked my head around the rim of the tub. It lay untouched, beside the mirror where I'd left it. I rested once more against the warm porcelain, though as I was leaning back I saw a flash of something reflected in the mirror. It was a figure in shredded rags and a grey snag of hair dense as cobweb in a century-old tomb. I thrust a look over my shoulder, prepared to find some hideous phantom lurking behind Daeva in the low light, but saw only my pile of wet clothes. Daeva herself had moved away from the mirror and was now standing near the door. Her midriff was exposed and her bare legs, pale and smooth as marble balusters, were visible through the long and sheer fabric draped around her waist. I perceived other exposed features as well, and understood then why she had come and what her intentions had been, intentions that I had rebuffed.

"I am sorry to have intruded upon your privacy," she whispered, ablush, and I felt a brute indeed when I saw the tears in her eyes. But before I could utter an apology she was gone, leaving me sitting in the bath crouching like a child with my hair plastered to my forehead and my heels digging into my buttocks. And I was shuddering; the steam had dissipated and the water had cooled considerably. The light had cooled also, changing the walls from pearl-glazed to the pitted grey of old skulls. It was as if Daeva had taken the room's vitality with her when she went.

I got out of the tub, my teeth clicking together uncontrollably, and crossed the slimy stone floor to the table where my suit had been set out. I took a towel from the stack, hesitated, then held out the sullied, threadbare length of material before me and let it unfurl. What did its frilled edges, its amorphous dark stains, its brittle texture remind me of? I did not dare sniff it. Groaning, I tossed the thing aside, pulled the suit over my damp and trembling frame and gathered the case and shoulder sack from beside the mirror. As I passed it, I glanced one last time at my reflection. It was depressingly normal again, though I admit I felt some relief in this. The steam was still receding from the glass, and as I looked then I noticed something unusual about the patches which remained. They resembled faces, their expressions variations of agony and despair, writhing as they evaporated. I leaned in closely to examine them but they were fading rapidly and were, alas, gone before I could discern any definitive characteristics, leaving me staring into my own reddened and shadow-ringed eyes.

I backed away from the mirror and moved toward the door, gazing stupefied around the room. It was so cold then that I could see my breath when I exhaled. The once-radiant globe was a lightless and hollow shell, and the tub stood like a rancid trough, the standing water cloudy and skimmed with a foul grey scum. Had I actually been *submersed* in it only minutes earlier? It seemed incomprehensible. A violent chill ran through me, forcing me backward out of the room, from which I fled as if from an image in a nightmare.

Entering the stair hall, I started in the direction of my room, then changed course and went instead to the library. I wanted to bring my father his new bottle of palliative serum. Also, after the disturbing episode in the bath, I admit that I did not want to be on my own.

The old man was seated at the hearth across from the bed, watching the flames bend and sway like trees in a tempest. The room was plush with warmth, and I felt at once soothed by it as I crossed to the table, where another service of magnificent cuisine lay untouched on one of those impeccably polished silver trays.

"They're going to start wondering why we are not eating," he said as I approached. Then, eyeing the shoulder sack: "What have you there?"

"Ingredients. They are bare, though at least palatable," I replied as I set the sack between the tray and a pile of handsome gilt-lettered volumes from Teethsgate's prodigious library. The items (those that hadn't fallen out through the tear) looked pathetic and unappetizing lying there in a pile, but once I had gotten the pot from my father's trunk, cut the vegetables and added the meat, barley, some spices and dried herbs from his stores and had it all simmering with fresh water from the basin, the lovely scent of a plain but hearty porridge filled the room. My father rejoiced at the sight of the full bottle of tincture. I poured beer for us (I tried to convince the old man to open the bottle of port given to him by the king from his own stores, to no avail), and we sat sipping it as rain battered the castle and the contents in the pot bubbled and thickened over the curiously smokeless fire. He asked about my journey to the village; I did not tell him about the fog, but I did relay the bizarre details concerning its oddly vacated aspect, including the missing broadsides, the unattended shops, and the children poking around like rats in ruins. I told him how I'd played for them, and about the woman who had stopped to scoff at me. To my annoyance, he thought this rather humorous.

"Your first detractor!" he said with a laugh.

"I did not find it so amusing," I said. "I have never been regarded with such unconcealed loathing."

"Well, as the saying goes, my boy, you cannot please everyone."

Irritated, I got up and began to set the table. As I was carefully moving the stack of fine books to the nightstand beside the bed, the old man said, "You needn't be delicate with those."

When I asked what he meant, he told me to open one. I picked up the first book, bound in dark green leather with sprigs of gold-leaf detailing and its title and byline embossed in silver. The spine cracked as I lifted the front cover, as if it had never before been opened. The cream laid flyleaf was blank. I turned it and saw that the frontispiece and title pages were the same; so too were those that should have contained the dedication and table of contents. I gripped the bulk of the manuscript in my hand and flipped through it—not a single word or numeral printed throughout.

"They are all as such," my father said.

"*All* of them?" I said, picking up another in disbelief and finding it the same.

"All but one ..."

The old man reached inside his coat and drew out a slim black volume which he presented to me with care. Unlike the others, this one was fragile, brittle, and much smaller. It was also extremely old; a smell of mildew wafted off it like the breath of ghosts. There was neither a title nor an indication of the identity of its author, only a small symbol embossed on the front: a rook in profile standing on what appeared to be a chunk of faceted stone. I ran my fingers across it, feeling the cracked leather flake beneath them.

"I have seen this before," I said. "In the garden. This hieroglyph is carved into a stone door there."

"Where is this garden?" he asked.

"In the courtyard behind the castle. The lady Daeva and I walked there yesterday," I said. I saw him raise his eyebrows as I opened the book. The pages were identical in format, with perfectly ruled lines of words penned in a rune-like alphabet, the letters of which resembled smashed spiders.

"It is written in Old Clænish," my father said. "They are essentially representations of our letters replaced with symbols. It was utilized as a form of military code, though subsequent generations adopted it as their primary written language for official documents and the recording of traditionally oral histories. The cipher for decoding it is simple so long as you know first which rune or grouping of represents which character. From there, go back two letters if it is a consonant; for vowels, look at the marking above the rune to determine which of the five it is."

"So what does it say?" I asked.

"It is a fairy tale," he said, threading his fingers over his pronounced belly, "about a refugee people who came to these shores from across the sea. They assumed the form of sable carrion birds, built a fortress, and conquered the region utilizing a powerful tool of their own forging referred to only as 'The Cold Flame.'"

I closed the book and gazed behind me at the towering shelves of tomes, all of which were presumably blank. "You found it amongst those?" I asked.

"It was in the stack that you brought to me," said the old man.

Frowning, I stared down at the bird emblem for a long moment, brooding on what it was reminiscent of. At length, I asked my father if he had seen a man in the concert hall during the performance on the night of our arrival.

"I don't recall. What did he look like?"

"Sallow of visage, with black eyes and hair. He was properly attired, though his clothing was worn and ill-fitting," I said.

"I saw no one other than our hosts," he said.

I nodded, handed the book back to him and then dished the porridge into a pair of teacups appropriated from the service cart. After the addition of several dollops of salt, it was actually quite sapid. We ate without speaking for some time. Then, as we were spooning the third helping from our minuscule vessels, my father said:

"The lady Daeva fancies you, then?"

"How should I know?" I replied.

"Do you fancy her?"

"Oh, come now, Father. She's only a girl," I said, though my words to my own ears lacked conviction. The image of her standing at the door in the *salle de bains* not an hour ago, bare beneath her gauzy wrapping, had not been without salacious regard.

"Precisely," the old man said. "It is therefore unwise to utter that which might be mistaken as promise. Nor should *you* rely on any uttered by her, for the allure of conquest is often twofold."

"Yes, yes," I huffed. I drained the ale from my glass, set it on the table and got up. "Do not worry, Father. I do not seek to kindle in others what is denied me."

"What does that mean?"

"It means that I'm tired. I think that I shall turn in early tonight," I said.

"And what about rehearsal? We have not mastered the andante," he said.

"One will have to suffice for today," I said and picked up the instrument case.

I had been intensely angered by the conversation, a feeling which contrarily increased the further I got from my father and the library of vacuous books. By the time I had reached my room I was in a rage, swearing and pitching my knapsack across the room. I held up the oblong box before me, cursed, and tossed it onto the table where I am presently writing this. When it struck I was myself jolted, shoved to the floor as if by phantom hands. A dissonant hum sounded, resonating not only from the viola but my own bones in the form of marrow-deep pain. Tears blurred everything, spit and blood ran from one corner of my mouth. It was over in moments, though the aftermath of the agony was enough to keep me supine and gasping for several minutes.

When at last I did rise, I went to the table and opened the case. The viola was the shade of a livid bruise in the burnt-orange moonlight passing through the arched window; I touched it and that needle tingle of pleasure ran injection-like into my arm and through my afflicted body, throbbing in sensual waves.

I can recall the first time I felt that peculiar sensation. I was in my eleventh year, and not at all a paradigm of the word "prodigy." In truth

I was, at best, a fair player, for I was not infatuated with music. Poetry was my love. I read it insatiably and had even begun to compose bits of my own juvenile verse. (I recall that our little hamlet's chaplain found them most promising). My father wouldn't hear of it. He had sacrificed all to make me a great violist, and so I suffered through the hours upon days upon years of monotonous scales, vibrato exercises, and spiccato techniques. I despised them, but I detested more my father's disappointment as he gradually despaired of his son's talent—instead, a mediocrity which became increasingly evident with every passing year. Perhaps the old man had discerned this earlier, though by then he had already sacrificed his own vocation as a soloist in order to become my pedagogue. I could not comprehend why he had relinquished his own ambitions, especially since I showed no inclination toward nor possessed an inherent talent for music prior to inheriting the Inamorta.

The viola came to me less than a month after they laid my mother in the thawed spring dirt. I can recall the events of that day with eidetic precision, though I cannot be certain that the hue of memory was quite as warm as it was in reality. My boyhood house has taken on somewhat of a mythic quality in my mind, despite my father's and my shared grief and the fact that we were relatively poor while living there. In my recollection, brilliant April sunshine poured through the leaded glass of the mullioned front windows. I was sitting in a square of that divided light, reading a tract of love sonnets when my father came through the door with a gust of brisk spring wind and the oblong box under one arm. At first sight, I thought he had brought home a small coffin, and then I saw the locking mechanism and recognized it as an instrument case.

He bade me join him on the sofa and told me that he had just returned from the solicitor's where he had heard my mother's will and last testament read. Then he sat very still for a long time with the case on his lap, gazing at the portrait over the mantel. I asked if he was all right. He did not answer, only reached in the breast pocket of his coat and drew out a key. It was attached to a thin black cord that resembled what I imagined the intestines of some eviscerated night snake. He stuck the key in the lock, turned it, and lifted the latches. His hands trembled as he did this; I had never, and have not since, seen him filled with such trepidation … or was it excitement? He raised the lid and I saw it then for the first time: the charred face, the bone fist scroll, those inward turned f-holes that seemed to fix on me in that instant with inexplicable recognition, seemed to say *You*. I asked him: "What is it?"—a foolish question of course, to which he replied with an equally obvious response: "A viola." Then he added: "It belonged to your uncle, who was a renowned soloist."

I had been until that moment unaware that I had an uncle, let alone one who was a famous musician. I asked his name. "Albert von Glahn," my father said quietly.

"The legendary violist?" I said.

He nodded slowly, gazing at the floor boards. I noticed that he had not once looked at the viola since opening the case. "He inherited it from his father who was a virtuoso, as was his father before him. You are the ninth male heir in a line of virtuosi whose progenitor is the viola's maker himself. As your grandfather had no male heirs, your mother was entrusted as its steward until you reached an age suitable for claiming it or upon … her … death."

I asked what had happened to my uncle. My father swallowed hard and pressed the back of his hand to his mouth. The hand shook as he lowered it. He said that von Glahn had "met with an unpleasant end," and disclosed no further details. I was listening to all this while staring at the viola. It was as if the oblong box resting on my father's lap was a family vault which, now opened, was pouring out all sorts of buried family secrets. I could see that bony, avuncular finger pointing at me, singling me out from beyond the grave. I was chosen, predestined, and in my eyes the blackened thing before me was suddenly an object of frail beauty, dependent now upon me for its care and protection. "It must be exceptionally valuable," I said.

"Indeed, it is priceless," he whispered.

I frowned then, recalling several occasions during which I had heard my mother and father discussing matters of money with great distress. "But why did Mother not sell it?"

My father looked up at me. "It was not hers to sell. She was but its ward; *you* are its predetermined inheritor. However, her provision comes with a clause: she advises that you should never play it. In fact, she implores you to destroy it."

I was dumbfounded. "Why would Mother take such care in preserving it only to have me destroy it?"

"These are matters of which I am not consented to speak of. It is my duty only to counsel you as her proxy, and her advice was for you to annihilate the instrument." I said that I would not. "I will not constrain you to honor your mother's wishes," he said, lifting the case and offering it to me. "But know that in accepting this instrument, it becomes your ward, your burden."

Burden. I thought it a curious word at the time. I do not now. I studied my father's expression as he handed me the oblong box as if it were an infant. There was resignation there, and also, what was it...? was it *hope*? In hindsight, this suggested a decidedly shadowy attribute of his character, for I sensed no reluctance in him, and he did not attempt to convince me further. Perhaps there were other motives, financial being not the least, for holding his tongue. He had, alas, not the convictions of my mother, nor as I would come to learn, any instinct for my welfare.

I carried the cumbersome case to the square of sun where my book of poems lay. Despite the light shining directly on the viola I saw no reflection, no sheen. It was as flat-black as tar. I lifted it out, along with my uncle's bow, and stood. The instrument was almost comically large; it is nearly eighteen inches—large as violas go—and I was undersized for my age. I can recall feeling ridiculous holding it to my neck, realizing that I would barely be able to reach first position. With my father watching raptly and, it could be said, acquisitively, I raised the bow and brought it down on the strings.

It was like a detonation going off within me. My vision went red as if my head had stuck the stone, and simultaneously streaming tendrils of sea floor cold flowed through my limbs. They located my functioning heart and usurped its rhythm ... and—it was a hand, wasn't it? yes!—that hideously fist at the top of the viola's neck, squeezing and releasing, regulating the surge of cooling blood through my newly denominated vessels and cerebral cortex as it propagated its will to my fingers and my bowing arm. Music filled the room like a forbidden language, raw bellows of grief and rage that distempered the soul to suffer, and rising above it, blotting the sunlit window like a doomsday eclipse was a head black as crematory smoke with ragged and hair hacked as if from a dead horse. Superimposed over this was my own small skull—I watched my jawbone gaping as I screamed and screamed in counterpoint to the insane torrent of notes pouring from the belly of the instrument. I could not let go—I had no control, and as my viscous blood began to slow and clot I knew that death was near. And then, as if the sensation was merely the figment in a nightmare, the chill evaporated and the pain was supplanted by a singular sense of euphoria which I would not experience for several years hence as everything on my body stood erect and I was released, fully.

When I next looked at my father I saw him regarding me with one tremulous hand covering his mouth. He was weeping. I had never seen him cry, not even during his mother's funeral; as a proper man of his time, his emotions were always rightly suppressed. It startled me. I dropped the viola and bow and threw my arms around him. He held me as well—a rare instance of displayed paternal affection—though there was something remote about his embrace, for it was reciprocated not in tenderness but *relief*. His last decade of work had not been in vain after all; the boy *would* be a genius, with all the praise and prominence and wealth that went along with it. And yet was I not equally egoistic, contemplating in that same moment with timorous awe the inestimable faculty I had just inherited?

Later that night after my father was asleep, I crept downstairs with a candlestick in one hand and the oblong box in the other. I sat in a wingback chair before the recently extinguished fire, above which that blocky and pasty likeness of my mother hung, and raised the lid. The viola was there, like the face of some unfathomable creature surfacing on a midnight sea. I hesitated, eventually found courage, and plucked the open C string.

Joshua Rex

The note was clean, round, unwavering, and resounded this time without the pain. It was above all a voice, a hum not unlike that of my mother's—a velvet carapace. I plucked it again and again while gazing up at that irregular likeness gratefully, so very grateful was I to her for this one final gift. As I write this now, I wonder whether her real "gift" had been the one which I squandered: her edict to destroy it, her attempt to save me from this cursed life.

Melania's Tale

(I have decided to record the following herein, since I am the only survivor to know it and have reason to do so. It was made known to me not through oral account but as if in a dream; though rather unlike a dream it remains in my memory as if it were my own: that is to say, as if indeed I had lived it. And perhaps now it is mine, deprived otherwise of a primary host and forever inculcated as it is in my recollection. As for its protagonist: *requiescat in pace et non reversus est.*)

❧

She was born Melania del Corvo, *a field hand who lived with her father and three older brothers in a single-room shack a mile from the city walls. While a revival of art and music flourished within these, beyond them thrived only the hardscrabble life of the peasant. Fourteen hours a day, six days a week they toiled in the wheat fields owned by Signor del Barberi, the feudal lord of the region. When Melania wasn't separating kernel from chaff or pitching hay onto a dilapidated cart, she was at home mending the clothes, tending to the animals, preparing the scant meals, and scrubbing the crude cookware. Her mother had caught a chill three winters past and died wrapped in filthy rags on louse-infested straw. The ground had been too hard to bury her, so her sons had wrapped her in a sack and packed her body in snow behind the cottage until the first spring thaw, but the wolves found her beforehand. After that, all of the domestic duties had fallen to Melania, the only daughter. If she failed to* complete these tasks, it fell to her brothers to punish her at their discretion, and by whatever means.

It was a life of soul-dimming drudgery in which an imaginative and precocious girl existed primarily in the private fantasies of daydreams. Every day, usually at sunrise or sunset during her walk to or from the field, she would gaze across the golden waves of wheat to the ringed cluster of buildings in the distance, their terracotta roofs warm in the waxing or waning sun, and her mind would fill with visions of what it was like there. These were fantastical imaginings, to be sure (neither Melania nor her kin had entered the city), formed out of the necessity of distraction from suffering and ennui. She saw people pale as marble dressed like gods in golden fabric that billowed and fluttered like bird wings. They were artisans and storytellers, magicians and actors and musicians. They walked down diamond-paved streets; their fountains were graced with sensual figures cut from crystal and ran with water cold as blue ice; they ate feasts which were gastronomical masterpieces and drank wine which produced only good cheer in its imbibers. The animals that roamed the tortuous lanes of sun-warmed stone were courteous creatures with wizened expressions. These even spoke and sang, and the songs they produced were of the pensive and mellifluous sort, full of myth and laced with velvet ribbons of tune which lilted and lulled in mystic choruses beneath the coruscating moonlight.

Beyond the walls, in the hard and godless countryside, there were no songs other than hers. These strains, borne of her anguish and delivered through the flawless vehicle of her voice, were formed like clay upon a potter's wheel, rendered gradually from raw and elemental material into exquisite form through emotive permutation and the addition of accentuation and inflection. Her accompaniment was exclusively the sizzle of insects under the broiling sun, the ocean rush of leaves, and the atonal bleeps or maddeningly recurring ravings and laments of birds.

When she was a girl her father had delighted in her ability, when her trifles were merry and bell-crisp. As her voice deepened, acquiring a lusty depth with age and burden, he would at once order her to cease, with threat of violence should she recommence.

She continued to sing in the field, however, until the day her voice drew through the sea of wheat a boy from a nearby farm. Melania was no longer a girl; though slight, her body was lean and curved. Her skin, when sweat-dampened, resembled glazed bronze, and her hair and eyes were soil-black. The boy had asked her name. She did not respond, though her heart had quickened in his presence. Her eldest brother appeared then with the knife he used to castrate sheep and chased the boy off. Thenceforth Melania was forbidden to sing (the defiance of which meant the removal of her tongue) and thus woeful were the mute sunlit hours of the interminable years to follow. But when her father and brothers slept, she would often sneak away and venture far from the cabin, following the river toward the city where she would let rush forth all of the stifled sentiment like black water bursting a dam.

During one of these surreptitious outpourings, as she sung in a low tone a minor key canzone while regarding herself in the reflection of the swollen moon on the surface of the river, a man in a black cloak appeared suddenly behind her. Before she could scream, he had one soft-gloved hand locked upon her mouth. Despite struggling with much vigor, she was carried off easily toward a copse where a carriage waited. Into this she was thrust, the door was closed and latched behind her, and without hesitation it began to speed away.

Melania shrieked, howled with feral rage, kicked at the door again and again to no avail. In her thrashing she did not see the man seated across from her in the cabin, and upon noticing him fell altogether still and silent. He possessed a round and craggy visage from which protruded a sharp and prominent nose. This was framed by two wavy plaits of silvery hair extending from beneath a flat cap of burgundy velvet. He wore fine clothes and smelled woody and of warm stone, with a hint of honey sweetness beneath. His eyes, like two moss-covered stones, were fixed on her as if she were a rare animal he had ensnared. He introduced himself as Giovanni, a Cremortan maker of viols. He then asked for her name, to which she gave no answer.

"I hope that you will forgive my driver's impertinence. He is ignorant in the use of etiquette concerning the proper treatment of a lady."

His intimidating stare was disparate from the refined and gentle way in which he spoke, and despite the rough manner with which she had been handled, Melania found herself relaxing into some mode of ease, for she had never been addressed with such kindness and deference. A lady, he had called her!

"I have listened to you many nights from behind the city walls," he revealed. "You have indeed the most singular alto I have ever heard." He paused, then added: "Are you frightened of me?"

She shook her head.

"I am glad to hear it, for I would like to make you my wife, should it please you."

Melania stared at him, utterly without words.

"You need not provide an answer yet. In fact, you needn't say a thing, so long as you agree to sing."

He laughed then—the sound was like a blade sawing through a tree, and it startled her. In the next moment she was distracted by a blush of flame in the coach's window. She watched with unmitigated awe as the carriage approached and then passed through the massive doors of the torch-flanked entrance to the city.

There were no gods in flowing white gowns, no wise and noble fauna, and the streets were not paved in crushed jewels. The people were less decorous than she had imagined, though nonetheless comely and fastidiously dressed in elaborate and bright clothing, their hair scrupulously styled. The carriage passed along staid and salubrious cobbles—no mud or animal filth here—past magazzinos filled with bounties of fruit and meat and bread and fine wares; beer merchants, cobblers, chandlers, a smithy and a tailor. The buildings had towers and arcades, stained glass, and iron rails that curled like vines.

They crossed a bridge spanning the river's course through the town, passed beneath another which connected the upper levels of two buildings, and at length stopped before a three-story palazzo of coral-colored stone. A pair of footmen waiting out front came forward and opened the doors of the coach, and Melania was assisted out by Giovanni himself, who guided her through the entrance and into a candlelit foyer, where they mounted a grand white marble stair to the second floor and crossed over the threshold into the first of a suite of rooms, which the master stated now belonged to her. There was a four-poster bed of ornate oak draped in blue fabric; silver-framed mirrors; white woolen rugs; and a vanity with a toilet and accoutrement worthy of a Contessa. In the doorway between the two rooms stood an old woman in maid's dress. The master instructed the latter to "see to the ablutions," and turned to depart. Melania, panicked at the prospect of being left with the washerwoman, gripped Giovanni's arm. He appeared amused by her panic.

"There is nothing to fear," he told her gently. "Entrust yourself to Portia, and I will come for you later."

Portia, whose speech was coarse and blunt as Melania's, led her to the second room, in which stood a large porcelain tub steaming with rose water. The windows had been opened here, and the night air, tinted with fire smoke and the scent of the day's sun-baked clay roof tiles, wafted through the sheer drapes, which hung long and unrestrained. After much coaxing, Melania allowed the woman to peel off her grubby field dress and grotty underthings, and when she slid into the bath it was with an involuntary and trembling sigh that was almost a groan. The water turned grey at once, and then a soupy brown as Portia scrubbed Melania's crusted scalp and nails and the hair under her arms.

After, the woman wrapped her in a pale robe, and before departing, showed her to a armoire where hung several exquisite garments. Beneath these were lined several pairs of silk and leather chopines. Melania dressed in a modest white shift and then walked to the open windows, outside which she saw a narrow balcony. She stepped out onto this and stood for a long while surveying the lustrous city and its perimeter wall, arcing like the bright rim of a planet. Beyond this was a void of darkness in which land was inextricable from sky. She knew that the fields were there; the olive-and-cypress-stenciled countryside and the vast undulations of wheat. How very distant it already seemed. She saw in her mind the tiny shack where her father and brothers now slept and imagined them wakening to her empty bed and subsequently stalking her through the woods and fields like dogs trained to track the scent of blood. They would never find her, though—not here—never would they suppose anything like what had occurred. Perhaps they would suspect the boy from the neighboring farm. Melania shuddered in consideration of what they would do to him.

And yet the terror that she felt was residual and nothing more, for looking down past the orange roofs to the slow shuffle of the people below in the vermicular streets, and the bend of the river as it flowed under the ponti and past quays, she understood that she had crossed not only the border of the city, but one which separated two modes of life. Time was not a curse here, nor days suffered through; rather, they were passed leisurely and pleasurably. There was continuity and the possibility of introspection, and freedom from fear. It was indeed a wholly new place, a new chance, and it was presented to her on the merit of her greatest gift. Recognition of her sudden independence coursed through her with the fervor of wine, and she wanted nothing more than to sing now—a canzone of liberty that would silence the thrum below and rake the night birds from their branches in the obscured lands beyond, but she demurred instinctively.

Some while later, she was brought a silver tray containing a feast unlike any she'd beheld. There were grapes and figs, a platter of salmon, cakes, nougat with honey and almonds, and at the center of it all a small roast bird—its cooked skin only a shade darker than her own. She sat upon the floor as was her home custom and, eschewing the flatware, utilized her hands to devour every speck of the feast. Made subsequently somnolent by the richness of the meal and its immense portion, she laid down upon the bed and was asleep almost instantly.

Some hours later she was woken by the click of the door latch. Melania sat up in the black room, ignorant of her whereabouts and petrified then by the appearance of a solitary flame floating toward her—first seemingly disembodied, then attached to a candlestick held by a phantom hand which, at length, revealed itself as belonging to Giovanni Morturia. He wore a long nightshirt and his head was lowered as he approached the bed, the hair hanging in stringy sallow bands. She saw in his eyes the same intent that had been in those of her eldest brother two years prior to her first blood. Bewildered, she had not fought then but she did now, with all her will, and was throttled for it. Thereafter she lay still, and once he had had his pleasure, he informed her that should she resist him again she would be bound, and that her suffering would be prodigious. He then departed, leaving Melania raw and alone and wishing that she were back at the river.

In the dour and sunless morning there was another knock. It was a servant this time, come to tell her that the master had summoned her to his atelier. Melania followed the man downstairs, along a series of stately corridors, and finally through a door that opened onto a large room which was austere and rustic in comparison to the rest of the house. There it was warmer, more humid, and the air was redolent of wood and that honey-sweet scent she had smelled in the coach. Along the left wall were several windows and a long bench where sat a half dozen silent and taciturn men, each carving the same object with the intense concentration of monks laboring on illuminated manuscripts. Melania did not know what these objects were, though she conjectured they were some form of musical apparatus. At the center of the room was Morturia, seated at a table larger and taller than the others and examining a pair of rectangular boards. Its surface was cluttered with papers and rags and fine tools and jars containing liquids of various shades of brown and red. Upon Melania's entrance, he barked gutturally, "Leave us," which the men did without hesitation, rising in unison and quitting the room with neither a glance at her nor Morturia.

When they had gone, he set down the wood he had been considering and stared at her for a long while without speaking. Melania found herself trembling like a wet dog with those eyes upon her, and the memory of the previous night still in sensation, and fear tangibly close. She gasped when he suddenly rose, and took down one of the curved apparatuses from where it hung alongside a number of others on a cord tied taut between two walls. This one had strings. Morturia turned and faced her and strummed these with his thumb, producing an ascending set of most alluring chimes not wholly unlike a human voice.

"Do you know what this is?" he asked. She shook her head. "It is called a viola. Of all their makers, I am the greatest." He then picked up off his table a bent stick strung with a white band of hair, which, after raising the viola to his neck, he drew across the strings. Music—the first melody she had heard other than her mother's voice—filled the workshop like a gust of wind through an open window. Morturia was not a great player; indeed, he was hardly a competent one, but she was nonetheless mesmerized by the sound flowing forth like alien language. When he had finished, he set the instrument aside and said:

"Now I would like you to sing."

Her blood seemed to stop in her veins. Her hands rose inadvertently, covering her mouth, as if in fear he would violate this as well, drawing out through force the single essence of herself preserved and protected for no one other than herself.

"I said I would like you to sing for me," he repeated. When she remained thus without reply, he said darkly: "Was the bath not of a pleasing scent and temperature? The dress not of your particular style? Did you find the food unpalatable?" She shook her head vigorously. "I am pleased to hear it, and yet I ponder why in spite of these offerings you should refuse to oblige my only request...."

"I know no song, signor, other than my own," Melania said.

"That will serve. And you shall address me not as signor but Master henceforth."

"Yes, Master," she said. She chose then a song from her mental catalogue—a dolorous air hummed in private commemoration on the anniversary of her mother's death.

Her voice was sudden thunder in the room—bold and umbrous and profound and as always, totally under her control. It was inextricable from her flesh, an organic force of nature; it had no Master—not even Melania herself could claim what merely Was, existing without training or honing. She comprehended these notions to be axiomatic at the dirge's crescendo; and it was a power, this revelation that Master though he might be, Morturia could never truly possess her or her instrument.

Morturia regarded her silently and with a slight look of shock, as if the song had been a phantom he had seen suddenly materialize and disappear before him. His clenched hand trembled upon his bench, and there was a look in his mossy eyes of insuppressible awe, envy, and covetousness though when he did at last speak it was in a tone which belied these.

"Again. This time something with more pace and articulation."

Melania did not understand, and said as such. The Master demonstrated in his crude playing an example of what he sought, and she comprehending then, obliged him. This mode of query and compliance went on for an hour, on the conclusion of which Morturia declared, after a span of contemplation and calculation and with neither ceremony nor any palpable affection, that they would be married the following night. He proceeded next to disclose to her the details of said arrangement, including the benefits she would enjoy as wife of a great luthier. He would purchase for her at her whim anything she liked—be it clothing, food, wine, jewelry, trinkets, furnishings—so long as she agreed upon two conditions: first—she would never for any reason leave the palazzo, and second—she would sing for him whenever he requested. In addition, he forbade her to reveal to anyone from whence she hailed, and should anyone inquire, he or she was to be told that she was the daughter of a noble, given to the Master along with her dowry in exchange for one of his much-coveted instruments.

And so they were married the next night, in a private ceremony conducted in an unused *salotto* with only the *prete* and Portia as witnesses. In the weeks after, the Master proved to honor his word. Melania was given anything she asked (a want which grew each time he departed for the city's many expensive *negozi* and *botteghe*), and in return, she honored his caveats. She remained inside the palazzo or within the confines of its resplendent gardens. And she sang for him—mostly in his atelier as he worked. As well, she endured nightly and submissively the excruciating physical renderings of his 'love,' though these were suffered not without an accruing cache of repressed fury.

As the months passed, gradually the miseries of her early life in the form of toil and want were replaced with benumbing ennui, shame, and melancholy. She came to regard the house as her prison, and its Master her jailor, though paradoxically she found herself desperate for his company and attention. Curiously and in proportion to the aggrandizement of these sentiments, his interest in her seemed to diminish steadily. His countenance turned sour in his wife's presence, and he scoffed reproachfully at her fine clothing and adornments. His interlocutions with her became increasingly sparse, and he called upon her to sing with less and less frequency until at last she was prohibited from entering his atelier. Even his nocturnal visits to her bedchamber ceased; this she regarded as merciful, to be sure, though the absence of his "attention"—brutal though it was—she observed with a conflicting sense of regret.

When after several months her languor and loneliness had mounted to the point of desperation, Melania descended to the atelier one drear and grievous afternoon in search of the Master. She would plead with him for emancipation, would herself renounce all ownership of the many acquired luxuries given by him, and promise never to trouble him or speak of him to anyone should he be so magnanimous as to grant her a release outside of the city walls. Reaching the door, she tried the handle with a quavering hand and found it unlocked, and in the next moment brazenly entered.

The Master was not within, nor were any of his apprentices. Alone she had never been in the workshop, and as it was the only room in the palazzo within which she had not passed countless idle hours, she began to wander throughout, picking up and putting down tools and carved wood and the curious jars of auburn and amber and umber tinted fluids. She did not, however, dare touch any of the violas hanging by their scrolls on the cord strung above and throughout. Without the candles, and lit only by a grey, strained light which gave the panes the look of dirty ice, the atelier was gloomy and had an air of abandonment.

Melania approached the Master's table where she examined the many objects there: the silver blades, the chisels and gouges, the involuted plans on vellum. She was examining one of these pages when she heard the door open behind her. Her heart tightened in her chest like a fist as she turned, expecting the Master, but it was a young man whom she had never before seen standing in the doorway. He was perhaps her age—a field hand by the looks of his unstyled black hair, russet-colored clothing, and clay-brown skin, which, as her own once had, clung tight to bone and muscle from hunger.

"Mie scuse, signora, I am looking for the Master, Signor Morturia," he said softly, almost sotto voce.

"He is not presently at home," she replied. Her own voice sounded to her unaccountably authoritative and confident. There was as well a seductive quality therein, a dusky felinity. "Who are you?"

"I am the new apprentice."

Melania had not of course known that the Master had been taking any on, but she did not disclose this to the young man. Instead, she nodded as if his arrival had indeed been anticipated, and commenced querying him further. "Where are you from?"

"The fields, signora. Beyond the city. The Master offered my father many florins for my service...." He paused then, his eyes roaming the shop.

"I admit however that I am most baffled, for I have no experience in this trade."

"Do not fret," she said, moving toward him, "everything can be learned. I myself came from the fields."

He regarded her with astonishment. "You did?"

"Many years ago."

"But you are so fair, so ..." he broke off, gazing down at his cap held in his callused fingers.

"What is your name?"

"Pietro. Might I ask yours, signora?"

"Melania, la padrona di casa."

"The Master's wife?" She blinked her assent. "Mie scuse," he said again, bowing slightly.

"The Master will be along soon," Melania said. "You may wait here for him, though if you require anything, or should you feel homesick, know that you have a friend in this house." She touched his hand briefly as she departed; he looked up at her, and in his eyes she saw desire sharp and clear as a dazzling ornament. She left him there on the threshold of the atelier, climbed the stairs leading to her chamber in haste and threw herself upon the bed where she lay for nearly an hour intoxicated with ardor. She learned from a servant the following morning that Pietro had been installed in a room somewhere within the palazzo for the duration of his apprenticeship. This was indeed anomalous, as the Master's other pupils' movements were restricted to the atelier: they were not permitted to pass beyond even the doorway leading inside the house.

For the whole of the ensuing fortnight Melania slept little. Wakeful and fervent she was in her bed; in her mind she crept through the halls seeking him, her thrill and her need augmented with each quickening step until at last she came upon a door, beyond which he lay bare and in a tangle of sheets, his olive eyes beckoning. These rapturous visions became so intense she found herself desperate to appease them, and so when the Master informed her one afternoon of his spontaneously and imminent departure to the neighboring outer lands in search of tone wood, she hesitated only minutes after watching from her high window his carriage pass through the city walls before going in search of Pietro.

She found him in the atelier, and there on the floor they lay together without a single word spoken. It was the first of several such trysts—all occurring in the workshop so as not to alert the servants. After each fervid coupling, they would talk of their early lives and hardships, of the present circumstances and the tyrant they both called "Master." They discussed as well the possibility of fleeing, of returning to the fields where they would be free of his terrible rule and Cremortan decadence. Ineluctably Pietro would begin to touch her, and Melania him in response, and at length their shared torment was made null. Pietro, not Giovanni, became her master—one not of twine and rod but the heart alone.

They decided to abscond on the eve of the Master's return. Covered in a cloak and with only a sack of prudently selected provisions, she descended to the atelier around midnight. The palazzo was silent; for an instant she sensed foreboding in that stillness, though she did not allow it to quell her exhilaration. The workshop was lit by a single candle burning at Pietro's bench though she did not see him there. She became aware of a creaking sound in the shadows near the back of the room, steady like the rocking of a ship at sea. She beckoned to him but he did not come forward. She saw the dark outline of a figure in the charry gloom at the back of the atelier, and taking up the candle started toward it. The light moved along the floorboards like a spreading flame, illuminating a pair of hovering boots and russet trousers—the latter saturated with blood at their nexus—then arced to the rafters where hanging amongst the violas she beheld the livid head of her beloved.

A single clear note like a siren resonated the strings of the bodies suspended above her—suppressed in the next instant by a hand and the rag and the fumes....

19th November, 1799
After the Count's fête

The furniture is piled against the door; I have dragged all that could be there, though I have heard nothing stir in neither the corridor nor the rest of the castle despite the multitude of guests presumably lodging here this night. Tomorrow I shall return once more to Larmes Harbor in an attempt to hire a carriage, though I doubt any driver might be found. Until then, in fear of putting out the candle—indeed how can I, knowing now the dreadful truth?—I am in the hope that the movement of pen on parchment will aid somewhat in reducing my present nervous state. By the erratic and jerky appearance of my script it appears thus far to have done little in that regard....

The day commenced same as the previous two, with a rehearsal of the new piece (specific focus on the third movement) in my father's chamber, followed by an insubstantial meal culled from the remains of that which I had gathered during my venture to the village. Played furioso, the piece requires much exertion on the part of the performer, and was interrupted on several occasions by the old man's cough. Incidentally, he has downed nearly two-thirds of the tincture procured for him yesterday, to ever lessening effect (I speculate whether it has had ultimately a deleterious effect on him) and I reckon I would have to return this afternoon in search of another bottle, as well as some form of aliment on which we might subsist the remaining four days. After the first successful run-through of the piece in its entirety we broke for the morning. My father, without removing his shoes, threw himself onto the bed despite having risen only three hours earlier, stating that he felt much fatigued. He was asleep almost at once.

I departed Teethsgate around eleven with the torn sack and coat, in the pocket of which I stowed a pen-knife in case I were to encounter whatever preying thing seems to inhabit the fog. To think that such a tool might function successfully in the capacity of defense is indeed risible, but carrying it afforded me at least a modicum of comfort. It was, however, much less damp and misty than the day previous, and though the clouds were still of a leaden hue, the sunlight straining through the haze of condensing vapor bronzed the late autumn treetops, providing a semblance of warmth to which the soul might adhere in the otherwise bleak and coldly featureless landscape.

As yesterday, I kept along the border of the woods, fingering the tear in my topcoat as I walked. I pondered whether I should attempt to locate a tailor during this journey, and furthermore if such a repair could be carried out within the few hours I had before this evening's soirée, which was to be held in my father's and my honor as well as for the arrival of the Count's nephew, the Duke of Danesfall, who upon learning of our commission insisted on being present for the performance. I was informed of this by the old man just this morning, after he had been informed of it by the Countess, who had visited his chamber at a most early hour to ask whether this would be permissible on our part. As it always went in these matters, he assented without the courtesy of asking me, and thus I would be enmeshed in an evening of tedious introductions and banal chatter.

Attaining the village, I determined it advantageous to seek out a tailor first. It would allow more time, should I find one, to complete the work—assuming that it was accepted at all, coming as it was from a stranger like myself in a town apprehensive of such. After an unavailing scan of the shop fronts along the main thoroughfare, I chose at random one of the lanes leading from it and started up the narrow, cobbled way between the rows of two-storied stone or clapboard houses made unbroken either by their adjoining walls or high wooden gates. Down several of these paths I wandered, accompanied solely by that foreboding silence which reigns crypt-like throughout the town until at last I spied a cottage-like domicile near the end of one of the lanes. Above its entrance, hanging from a rusty bracket, was a plain sign that read:

SAFFREY'S, DRESS AND ALTERATIONS.

Though the front windows were dark, light glowed in the dormers of the upper level. I rapped on the door several times without reply, and after a brief hesitation upon the stoop, turned back toward the center of the village. I was several paces on when I heard the interrogative squeal of hinges followed by the ping of a shopkeeper's bell chiming in the dim alley like bright coins.

"What do you want?"

The voice was decidedly sharp and devoid of civility. I could not from the low and brusque inquiry alone determine the sex of its owner, and thus how great my surprise to turn back and see there the same scowling woman from the square. She was scowling at me again, her eyes demanding, her posture severely upright. Her dress was of crêpe or bombazine, the material satiny and black as her long, loose curls which were restrained by a single lilac ribbon.

"I've torn my coat," I said.

She looked down at the instrument case in my hand, then back at me. "I am sorry, but I cannot take on any more work at this time."

I pressed her on the matter: "This is my only coat, you see. I had an … accident yesterday."

"An accident …" she repeated.

"It is only a small repair. I'll pay triple your rate."

"It is not a matter of payment," she said and stepped back through the doorway.

"Have I offended you in some way?" I called.

She appeared on the stoop again. "I beg your pardon?"

"Yesterday in the square. You seemed disenchanted with my playing for the children," I said.

"I don't recall," she said.

I hesitated; it was clear she was lying, but why? Then, as I was about to speak, she said: "Why have you come here?"

"I've already said … the coat …" I replied.

"No, I mean, this village. Who are you?"

"My name is Jonas Layne. I am a violist. My father and I are here on a commission from Count Canis of Teethsgate."

"And this 'accident' … did it take place *up there?*" she said, her eyes cautiously flitting in the direction of the castle.

"Well, not precisely," I said.

She nodded slowly; she seemed to be internally debating something. She looked past me, then side to side and said: "Come in and let me have a look."

Her shop had the smell of a musty armoire. A long table was pushed against the front window on my right. I glanced at the neatly arranged items there: a heart-shaped cushion stuck with pins and needles of every size; a coiled tape measure the color of corn silk; a woven basket filled with thimbles; an abacus-like device containing rows of thread spools; several hand-drafted patterns; and laid across it like a body ready for embalming was a little boy's suit of dark blue velvet and broderie anglaise. The small square of paper pinned to it was dated a month earlier. I saw a rack of similar tagged garments—her presumed backlog of repair work—along the southern-facing window, amongst which were a wedding gown and a christening dress. A staircase stood in the center of the room, leading to the second level where I presumed she resided.

I set the instrument case on the floor, took off my coat and showed her the torn lower left panel. She sat with it at her work table and spread the damaged section out beside the little suit. Her fingers traced the ugly gash, grazing it, gaping it, smoothing it again. Watching her handle with such care an intimate belonging of mine filled me with a singular and inexplicable pleasure.

"How did it happen?" she asked without looking up.

I told her that I snagged it, adding no supplementary detail. She nodded, brow furrowed, and said nothing. As she set the panel down I noticed that her hands were trembling.

"Leave it with me. I will have it repaired within the hour," she said.

"That is most kind of you, though I feel impudent in delaying your more pressing affairs," I said.

She looked forlornly down at the child's suit and said: "Just see to it that you return."

I thanked her, bewildered and somewhat disturbed by her cryptic words, and went out again into the blustery afternoon, heading in the direction of the square. The sky was the color of dirty bath water, as if the world were wrapped in a film of scum the sun could not penetrate. I walked to the corner shop, which since yesterday had been plundered further. Beneath a row of bins I found a couple of shriveled potatoes and tin of pickled fish, but no more bottles of my father's tincture. I cursed myself for not taking two upon my first visit. I stowed the pathetic spoils in the shoulder sack and tied it at the rip.

The scouring of the shop took only ten or so minutes. With a good three-quarters of an hour left before I could pick up my coat, I decided to explore the waterfront. It was even more tumbledown and decayed than I had perceived on first glimpse. Nothing there stirred save for several white crows, which alighted from slimy pilings as I stepped onto the boardwalk. The wind was quite bitter and carried with it the reek of putrefying fish and crustaceans. As I walked up and down the groaning piers I spied traps tied alongside the vacant trawlers containing dozens of the poor creatures left to roast helplessly in the high afternoon sun. Regarding them gave me pause. What had caused the men to hasten from their ships, loaded as they were with several days' catch? Furthermore, *why had they never returned for it?*

The boardwalk dead-ended at a tavern. Chilled without my overcoat, I sought shelter there, and was not surprised to find the door forced in. Like the provisions store, the contents were looted. There was a path of overturned tables leading to the cage bar whose posts had been broken, and the jugs and casks they had once protected pilfered. I went to the bar and peered through the splintered gap. I saw not a single vessel, though I noticed that the latch on the narrow door leading behind the bar was undone from the inside. Within I searched the shelves and discovered, obscured by the shadows in the lower left corner, a brown and label-less bottle which upon retrieving and uncapping, I sniffed the unmistakable fumes of whisky. This I added to my satchel, re-knotting it as I turned back to regard the grime darkened tables. Upon them were mugs filled with ale or liquor, pewter plates of rotting fruit, half-eaten bread, and molding cheese. The tallow candles had been left to burn and melt and had done so, running over their holders and drying like magma on the wooden surfaces. Everything about the scene suggested sudden flight.

Returning again to the center of the village, I came upon an object I had not previously noticed: a child's shoe. I crouched to examine it, then scanned the square but saw no children, nor were there any faces, distrustful or otherwise, glaring at me from under the eaves. It was then I realized that I had seen not a single individual other than the seamstress during my hour or so of exploring. I laid the shoe back on its side as I had found it, and started back toward the tailor's. The route led me past the wall of *Missing* notices. Some had blown off, carried beyond the wharf to the sea by the displacing wind. Of the faces that remained, one seemed to call to me as I passed. My hand trembles as I write this, recalling that moment of certain recognition. I tore the broadside from its tacks and hastily stuffed it beneath my tailcoat.

I was early in returning to the shop, though the repair was completed. The woman, whom I learned was the sole proprietor of the atelier and thus Miss Saffrey, said little as I paid the fee, only a parting warning to mind that I not "snag" it again.

I encountered no fog as I mounted the rise, nor, God be praised, was there any sign of the thing that had come out of it the day previous. I walked quickly nonetheless, keeping an eye on the dark border of the forest while fingering the new centipede-like bead of stitches through the silk lining of my pocket. As I inspected this, my fingertips felt something else at the bottom of the pocket itself: a piece of folded paper. It drew it out—a thin, folded tea-shaded scrap with deckled edges. Written on it in careful black script was:

It is not what it appears.

I halted on the bluff, repeatedly re-reading the message, my eyes moving slowly from one word to the next as if this would somehow force its implication up through the gaps in the letters and into comprehensible view. I could not determine why the seamstress had put it there, she who had reluctantly agreed to take on the repair and seemed much relieved indeed in seeing me depart. Nor could I derive any definite meaning from the fragment itself, though a vague inclination of insidious foreshadowing discomposed me as I returned the slip back to the pocket and continued on toward the castle. The keep, as it came into view, filled me then with sudden dread. I surveyed it with scrutiny, considering the size and scale and the decidedly austere exterior, though did not until some hours later comprehend precisely what in that moment unnerved me about it.

I went alone to the soirée. My father had passed a miserable afternoon; his cough, which had prevented him from sleeping no more than a quarter-hour at a stretch, was now to my great distress bringing up copious globules of scarlet phlegm. He was covered in a cold perspiration, which had saturated through his clothing to the sheets of his bed. There was a strong and disagreeable odor in the room, like spoiled meat, which I assumed to be coming from beneath one of the silver lids of the dinner afternoon tea service. After assisting him in changing out of his humid coat, breeches and underthings and into his nightshirt and cap, I gathered the edible parts of the pittance I had collected earlier and arranged them on a salver. I must say they looked quite good indeed. This, as anticipated, inspired little enthusiasm in the old man, though the whisky brought a light of cheer to his pasty and dour countenance.

As he sipped it from the bottle, I said that I would stay to care for him rather than attend the evening's event. Of course he protested vociferously, insisting that I not only attend, but offer regrets for his own unavoidable absence, though stated in a way which would excite in the Count neither alarm nor worry.

To my dismay, the Duke had arrived accompanied by an entourage of decadent revelers. They filled the Grand Room; yet another of Teethsgate's esoteric chambers which I entered through yet another of the paneled mirrors in the foyer. It was a space similar to the stair hall, ringed by an arched gallery, though this time of white marble and limestone, which was accessible via a grand staircase on the north wall. The ceiling was a single seamless mirror. What other details? Flesh-tone tapestry bedecked in fringe, and bunting the color of clotted blood. The globe-sized orbs swirled with smoky light, like storms captured under glass.

As one of the presumed honored guests, I anticipated many tedious and elaborate introductions and speeches; ergo, I was flummoxed at being essentially disregarded from the moment I entered, save for one of the servants who offered me a flute of flat champagne that smelled of spoiled mushrooms. I absconded to an unoccupied corner from whence I pretended to sip the fizzing swill in my glass while considering the bizarre coterie before me. Never have I seen an assemblage clad in such a multitude of styles, discordant not only with the present era, but free of the delineation of *class*. I glimpsed in one minor grouping a buccaneer, a prelate, a soldier (complete with bayonet), a pauper, a medieval courtier, and a woman with a decorative ship in her hair. I surmised that this must be some form of bal masqué—or unmasked, rather, as costume here took precedent over the necessity of a vizard. I saw the Count and Countess (the latter's pannier so wide it seemed in jest) engaged in discourse with a regally attired man. Like the Count, he was garbed anachronistically in a silver doublet and long crimson cloak with Minerva trim. I assumed it must be the Duke. Whether the Count noticed me I was not certain, but the Countess acknowledged my gaze, only to redirect it to Daeva, who stood at the center of the space beneath the radiance of a massive globe chandelier, which burned with the molten hue of the sun.

She was speaking to a rake with disheveled hair, handsome features, and crisp yellow eyes. He wore a fine emerald suit with golden brocade that shimmered gently—just enough to keep the eye continually drifting back to him. In one large and square-shaped hand was a glass of sherry; the crystal vessel looked minuscule in his square fist, as if he could crush it to dust with the slightest clench, and yet he held it with controlled delicacy as he regarded Daeva. She in turn was gazing upon that handsome face with a look of uninhibited desire, while around them the well-dressed glimmered and gossiped; it was the typical mix of shapely calves, powdered cleavage, and salacious eyes wielded like weapons.

Here I may without chagrin admit envy, as well as a sentiment of betrayal at beholding Daeva's duplicitous cunning. I had entrusted confidences to her which I had not disclosed to anyone, and now stood there a jilted fool, watching her cast a lascivious spell upon this hapless rogue. I decided then to attempt a surreptitious exit, and was only a few steps from the door when I felt a hand lock hard onto my shoulder. I was next turned by it, and found myself looking into the rake's yellow eyes. So glistening were they, so satiny and saturated, as if the source of the color itself, that I for several moments could not look away. He grinned at my impertinence, and said in a voice as wooden as his grip, "You are the *maestro?*"

"I am Jonas," I replied.

"Jonas Layne, the great virtuoso. I am Danesfall. It is an honor to make your acquaintance," he said. My expression of surprise was replaced by a grimace as he let go of my shoulder and shook my bowing hand with such force I felt my bones compressing—indeed, I was on the verge of crying out when he, perhaps sensing my discomfort, released it. "I came as soon as I learned of the commission," the Duke continued. "Rare is the opportunity to behold in person one possessing of *true and irrefutable genius*. Clever indeed of Rufus to engage you privately."

"Private, my lord?" I said.

"To have you exclusively at his disposal—his 'prodigy in residence,' if you will. The Count is infamous for the flaunting of his affluence, and thus I am sure you have been compensated amply for agreeing to slog all this way to the back of beyond in order to perform one piece. Though there are of course other perquisites besides the purely monetary which one of your illustriousness might at his whim seek to satisfy...." He broke off, glancing over his shoulder to where Daeva stood speaking to the man in the red cloak.

"I'm not sure I understand," I said, refusing to bolster his brazen impudence.

"Oh, come now, Jonas. You would not have me believe that she did not throw herself into your famous arms the moment you set foot here. I admit I am most envious of your position." Danesfall drew near; when he next spoke it was in a low murmur. His breath reeked like a swamp. "I wonder if she might be inclined to accommodate the *both* of us this evening. No need to feel timid, *maestro*. In my case, it was a boy who was the first to, shall we say, *storm the duchy*. No doubt your travels have rendered you vastly experienced."

I only half comprehended what he was implying, for as he spoke the man in the ill-fitting black suit appeared, ringed in a veil of shadowy aura. He was less tangible than the first time I had seen him; indeed his flesh was almost translucent, the crowd visible both around and *through* him as he passed amongst them unnoticed. He paused near Daeva, glaring at her, and then, as if by aid of some magnetic pull, his gaze was drawn to mine.

"Do you see that man?" I asked.

"To whom the lady is speaking? That is the first Earl of Fraktur."

I began to say that it was the other man, the one in black, when the latter turned suddenly and strode toward a space where there were few revelers—and an instant later vanished as if behind a wall! I have considered this over and again and cannot to any end reconcile it. The Duke, looking uneasy, quipped then about phantoms, though his jest was not met with any reciprocation of humor by me. An awkward pause followed, broken by Danesfall who, receiving no attempt at further discussion with me and finding Daeva no longer conversing with the earl, said he should not like to leave his host so unaccompanied and sauntered back to her. I detested the smile she gave him as he approached, one almost vulgar in its insinuation. I placed my glass of untouched wine on the base of one of the immense veined columns and slipped from the room, unnoticed as the elusive man in black.

Beyond the doors of the Grand Room the castle was silent and dim. I crossed the mirrored floor and started through the stair hall in the direction of the library, seeing not a single person—servant or otherwise. The gloom there was like a haze which, oddly, seemed to shift and re-solidify into a defined image wherever I cast my eyes. Everything in my periphery was meanwhile indistinct, like a wash of white paint over a black surface, and beneath was ... what? I could not perceive, and only grew more irritated the harder I tried. I thought perhaps it was an illusion of optics, or a hallucination resulting from fatigue, for I was exhausted from my round-trip voyage to the village, and nagged by lewd images of the self-imposed nature of Daeva and the Duke of Danesfall together.

I found my father propped against his pillows, contentedly reading one of his travel-weathered volumes. The bottle of whisky stood on the table beside him, three-quarters empty. There was a faint rancid odor in the room.

"How was your evening?" he asked.

"Dreadful," I replied. "I see the same can't be said for you. Would you spare some of that?"

The old man reached for the whisky, nearly knocking it over. I caught it, then fetched a glass and poured myself a double dram.

"Top me off as well, my boy."

"I think you're quite topped off already," I said.

"Fiddlesticks!" he said, thrusting his cup at the bottle neck. I filled it, reluctantly, and settled into the chair across from the bed. "Did you give the Count my apologies?"

"I did not speak to him."

"What? You went, of course...."

"Indeed, though no one seemed particularly interested in my attendance."

"Didn't you attempt to engage them?"

"*Yes*, Father," I sighed. "I need no tutelage in the useless art of banter."

"I wish I could concur. Though of your many skills, repartee is one you've yet to master."

"I am content in that regard with retaining my status as novice."

The old man was shaking his head. "The position of an inherent isolate. How like your mother you are—remote and inscrutable, even to those whom love you."

"I am not keeping anything from you. I just have no interest in fashion or folderol. My *god*, what is that *smell*?"

"You know that such discourse is vital to our ... what are you doing?"

I had risen and was inspecting the area around the bed. The stench was stronger near the footboard where his legs lay half-covered. He was reaching for the counterpane but I grabbed hold of it first and ripped it back—

One evening while my mother was at her needlepoint she began to cough. The pastoral scene of horses and wheat and white house was sprayed with crimson. The terror in her eyes implied her fate. Looking upon my father's leg in that moment I was no less certain of his, and I brought a hand to my mouth—both in shock as well as to block the vile odor—as the first threads of fear began to entwine around my heart like tendrils of vine around a tombstone. The bad color began just below his knee, darkening all the way to the foot where three of the toes had gone black.

"Why didn't you tell me, Father?"

"What would it have mattered?"

"You might've been able to save your foot!" I cried.

"They can lop the whole leg off for all I care. It would be better than the ache."

"Do not say that," I said. The panic was rendering me breathless. "I'll fetch a doctor at once in the morning. Maybe he will only have to remove ... a few ... toes...."

The old man merely shrugged. "At least it is not my pedal foot. It will not keep me from the concert."

"The *concert!* The concert be damned!" I shouted. "I shall feign complicity with this farce no longer. We need to leave this place, at once. What is presented here as reality is, I believe, a shroud of the most horrific implications."

I took the *Missing* broadside from beneath my lapel and handed it to him. He regarded it a moment, then looked at me with befuddled inquisitiveness.

"I saw that man yesterday—*here in the castle!* The physical characteristics are identical, of this I am certain. Ostensibly he is one of the servants. He seemed to have been drugged." I paused then, knowing that what I was about to say would be perceived as extreme hyperbole. "Father, I think the Count is kidnapping the people of Larmes Harbor and forcing them into servitude."

"Oh, what nonsense indeed," he said, setting the sheet aside.

"Is it, though? Tell me, have you not asked yourself precisely how this colossal interior fits within the confines of a modest medieval keep? And the books—" I said, going to one of the shelves, taking down and paging through one volume after another and tossing them onto the floor—"why are they all empty? What of the food—" I went to the trolley, upturning the domed silver lids, which clanged loudly as they struck the floor—"why is it unpalatable ... hell, indigestible?" I gave the cart a hard shove; the contents slid off and crashed, disgorging a stinking mess onto the deep amber rugs.

"I know it is odd, all of it. But please, Jonas. Oblige a dying man," he said calmly.

"You are not *dying*. You require …" I was searching—for what I knew not. There was nothing to find other than the hideous putrefying truth lying before me. I was falling, with the certainty that I would hit, and already intuiting the precise acuteness of that pain. Still I could not let myself relent. "… you require the care of a physician, and rest. Yes—a respite from this nomadic life we've been leading."

"Do not call it that."

"Why not? It is no other. We're like a pair of damned gypsies traipsing across the continent!"

"We are *musicians*," he said, drawing himself up. "Anyone would give all to be in our—in *your* position. *You are the greatest musician in the world.*"

I looked down at the oblong case beside my chair. "How long we have lied to ourselves, Father…?"

He sat silent for a long while, then said plaintively: "What else would we have done? Would you rather us peasants, plowing the fields for a pittance? Slaves in a workhouse wool factory, eating our gruel in a tenement or shack sitting besides cow pats? Or perhaps you'd prefer a fourteen-hour day shoveling coke into a blast furnace, your lungs black with soot and thick with tubercular blood? There are plenty who are far worse off than you and I, my son. We must count ourselves amongst the few fortunate."

"Fortunate, right. For the unremitting spinal ache from that infernal carriage. For the nausea, the loneliness, the perpetual insomnia. I remember—do you hear me, Father?—*I remember*. We were not so destitute as you make it seem. Now, though, we have nothing. No friends, no home, no family. No love."

"We have each other, Jonas. My love for you has always trumped all in this world, even the love that I felt for your mother."

"You say that you love me, yet *you* were the one who put it in my hands. You did not have to bring it home, though, did you? You could have buried it, burned it, smashed it in the street. Mother knew to keep it away. That was her gift, *her* love. But you were besotted with ambition. You could not live with the sacrifice you had made, squandered on my mediocrity. And now you know what it has done to me, you know how it will end, and you are content knowing it so long as you are allowed to continue this vacuous existence."

"It would have come to you either way," my father said, his voice low and eerily without emotion. "Blame me if you must, Jonas, for everything, for all your ills and unfulfilled longings. But it was not *I* who put this curse on you. Rather, I've devoted *my* life to helping you bear it. And I have done my best. We have conducted our business on our terms, at our price."

"What a price it has been," I said, picking up the instrument case. I crossed the room, paused at the door and looked back. "Just answer me this, Father. Why have we never stopped? Why haven't we gone home?"

"One does not make a home among the dead, Jonas," he said simply. Then, pulling the white sheet up over his blackened foot, he picked up his book and returned to his reading.

The reverberations of the argument shook me to the extreme; so sunk was I in the bog of my own thoughts that I was hardly conscious of my ascension to the darkened second level until I saw something crawling toward me out of the shadows at the end of the hall leading to my room. Terror arrested me as if I were jerked back and held in its reins, and I found that I could not move, even as a figure began rise. It was Daeva. So surprised was I by her sudden appearance (not to mention her bizarre approach) that I asked, rather brusquely and with appropriated authority what she was doing there.

"Where did you presume I would be?" was her response.

I replied, "With Danesfall, of course."

"Why would you assume such?" she said.

"I saw you together, at the soirée...."

She drew near, pressed her bosom to me. "Oh Jonas," she said. "Do you still not *know*?"

Her kiss was slick and slightly cool and I returned it without compunction. Nor did I protest in the least as she led me away, past the door to my chamber and through another at the end of the hall where a fire burned as if in anticipation of our arrival. The walls were the color of diluted blood, with a bone-white chair rail. The furniture was a muted red, the bed cover and canopy trimmed in metallic pea-green. The ceiling rose to a sloping apex like that of a tent, and from this peak a chandelier made of entwined glass tubes hung; sunset light flowed through them like water; a sensuous, pulsing rhythm. There were vases of Lovers' Tongues on every table, and the cloying yet bitter attar pervaded the space like smoke.

Daeva half-reclined on the bed and began unfastening her gown. Her underclothes were sheer; beneath her bustier I saw two smudges of pale rose, and between them, spread out along her breast bone and rising up her neck, were the serpentine strands of that silver necklace with the large dull gem at the center, so in contrast with her fairness that it appeared a hole in her sternum. It seemed to stare at me like a great somnolent eye.

"I want you to see me. To know everything," Daeva said. She drew up her petticoat, beckoning me, and I moved toward her without hesitation, set the instrument case down beside the bed.

Ah! If only I had fled!

As she removed my clothing, I began to shiver without cease. I was most embarrassed by this involuntary reaction, but she only giggled. "You shudder as if you have *not* been invited to the beds of countless daughters of Counts, *maestro*," she said, pressing her lips to my bare flesh, her hand sliding beneath the rim of my breeches. I had indeed been granted such invitations—copious to be sure—though not one had I accepted until this night. The dexterity and intuitive sensibility of Daeva's touch confirmed forsooth that she had not been as steadfast as I in abstaining; and it is with great shame that I confess a total and unequivocal yielding to my want.

Upon recollection, I cannot be certain when the sound began. Initially I thought it one of Daeva's cries—a variation of her pleasure in my ear—though as it grew louder I heard in it suffering. This single lament increased to a chorus of whimpers and sorrowful moans, the keens of a thousand funerals all around me. Then, I had a sudden cutting sensation in my chest, as if I were being pierced with a scalpel.

Opening my eyes I was almost blinded by the gem at the center of her necklace. It was sun-bright, though the "light" with which it blazed did not seem to be light at all, rather it was fluid and viscous, composed of a material utterly foreign to my experience and thus it evades any possibility of tangible comparison. The room itself was as well coated in the singular, shimmering glaze. It coursed down the walls, the furniture, flowed through the illumination fixtures and crept along the rug. Yes, it was *moving* because it was composed of distorted and writhing figures, extended and manipulated like wallpaper to cover the space. The faces were elongated to appalling proportions, their tensile matter distended and stretched until amorphous; arms and legs bent at repulsive angles, tortuous, rearranged, plastered atop one another. To my horror, I saw a thread of the same substance coming out of my chest, drawn like a strand of twine and disappearing into the gem's crystalline depths. For a long time I stared down at this detachedly; half of me seemed somewhere else—perhaps part of the figures? I could still feel myself rooted in her, pushing senselessly as if I were a machine. I was being drawn out entirely, and with each tug above and below I was flooded with simultaneous agony and rapture so that when I released, it was with excruciating ecstasy. At the climax I saw Daeva gazing back at me, her eyes mirrors, her hair an electric tangle. This was only for a flash—in the next instant a scream vanquished all. There was no despondency in it, no pain, only a piercing and malefic rage. As it passed between myself and Daeva I was thrown backward with such violence I struck my head upon one of the bedposts and lay crumbled like a marionette against the footboard.

For several moments my lungs felt frozen, incapable of accommodating air. My viscera were a tight coil of agony. Slowly and gradually with determined effort I was able to intake small breaths of air and the knot began to relax. When my breath had sufficiently returned for me to attempt speech, I said: "What ... *is* it?"

Daeva grinned wryly from the opposite end of the bed, her dress a tangle around her waist, her stockings rolled down her legs like the skin of a molting snake. Her eyes smoldered like igneous clinkers as she lazily stroked the gem, whose color had returned to that lackluster shade of amber brown, inert as the eye of a dead animal. "A very curious object," she said. "Unassuming, yet powerful. You possess something similar, don't you Jonas? A thing of equal *capability*."

I shook my head. "No …"

"You think that people look upon you without doubt, without suspicion? Are you so blinded by your own fame that you would deny its very source?"

"*I* am the source," I said. "A lifetime of practice is at the root!"

Daeva laughed mockingly. "*She* is at the root, *maestro*. 'Death's Beloved'—as well as your own. And now, mine."

She scampered toward me, eyes glowing as she climbed atop me. Her hand grasped below, her eyelashes were centipede-like against my cheek. "Together we could live, unchanged from what we are today, and I'll let you do *anything*," she breathed. Mortified, I felt myself swelling in her hand as she guided me to where I had not yet been.

With one thrust of the arm I threw her off, grabbed the instrument case and my clothing and fled from the room without a glance back. I do not know if she followed me, scuttling through the black hall as she had across the bed. I bolted the door of my chamber and pushed my trunks and all of the furniture (save for this desk and chair) I was able to move in front of it where I now sit with the viola beside me—terrified for my father, and with no plan as to how we might escape....

20th November, 1799
7:35 AM

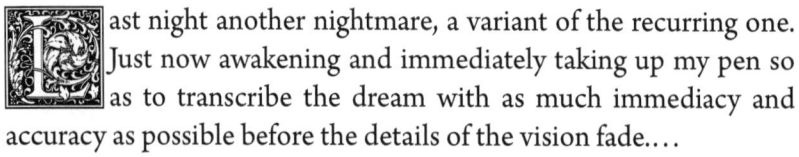

Last night another nightmare, a variant of the recurring one. Just now awakening and immediately taking up my pen so as to transcribe the dream with as much immediacy and accuracy as possible before the details of the vision fade....

Running through a series of dark tunnels with low, vaulted roofs. The chambers off them lined ceiling to floor with openings the shape of beehive ovens. A mess of bones throughout the corridors, crackling and skittering underfoot, dry as tinder sticks. Carrying a torch, though the hand which held it was not my own (black brocade sleeve, yellowed frilled lace) ... watching as if from a perch in someone else's mind (?) ... ignorant, however, as to his will ... in the other hand is a hammer and chisel.

After many turns, we reached a stagnant passage which terminates at a pedimented and bricked-over entrance. The man places the torch in a metal bracket beside it. A sound somewhere in the tunnels; a moan or a bay. He begins using the tools on the mortar, working fast, though the progress is slow, and he must pause often in his endeavor. At length a stone door is revealed, and at its center, a keyhole. A ponderous key is produced, slid in the lock and turned. The torch is removed. The man passes through the opening.

We are in a narrow space about the height and width of a large wardrobe with a depth twice that. The flame is held aloft, throwing garish light upon a solitary mummified corpse, its neck, wrists, and feet fettered to the stone wall. The face has gone to bone, though patches of recusant flesh still cling to the hands and legs. The figure is clothed in brittle robes; two long bands of snarled black hair hang from beneath the drawn up hood. The head, kept from falling to the floor by an iron clamp, is turned in such a way that it seems to be regarding us inquisitively.

The man kneels reverently before the body. I expect the eyeless gaze to follow us down but of course it does not. He speaks a name with an intoning of veneration—*Rainer*—asks pardon, rises, approaches. The torch reveals a braided leather cord around the shackled throat, at the end of which hangs a vertical silver pendant with two large openings the size of the orbital sockets of the skull. The man cuts the necklace free. (I shudder at the feeling of the husk-like cloth, the listless hair brushing the back of his hand as he places the pendant within his pocket.) He bows, backs away, bows once more—does not turn his back on that blank and angled stare until well outside the tomb.

Rushing through the tunnels again. The baying ... is near, seeking. Something flashes ahead and the man stops. Two openings in the dark where he sees himself twice reflected, though too distant for me to be able to determine identity. I begin to recede from his vantage down my own solitary burrow of black, and wake blinking out of darkness with my eyes upon the lancet, effulgent with the blood of the rising sun. Alack! What bitter panes—stretched taut as drums between the muntins—does that sanguine glow illume!

I must now make haste, for in addition to locating a physician and hiring a driver I have decided to again visit the seamstress. I believe she possess certain knowledge of this place, the obtaining of which is vital if my father and I are to survive the next twenty-four hours....

20th November, 1799
8:00 PM

It is one hour before concert-time, and I am at the desk in the library. The old man sits in an armchair in a mood of atypical introspection, his mind occupied neither by books nor dreams. We have not spoken since the decision reached earlier this evening, after my return from Larmes Harbor and my disclosure to him of the facts detailed to me earlier by Miss Isadora Saffrey concerning Teethsgate and its arcane family.

I have, to my immense shame, largely failed. My father has convinced me to honor our contract with the Count and perform the sonata, though only on my condition that we leave this castle at the first opportunity, *with no further engagements or commitments scheduled.* Presently, I know not by what *means* we will leave, as I was unsuccessful in my attempt at locating a driver in town. I must now concentrate my efforts on fleeing this wicked place. Prior to departure I shall burn this MS. For now I will continue to utilize it as a divertissement to pass the time before what is to be the last performance of the *"maestros"* Layne. I should add that I have written "last" without specific denotation, for in all truth I know not what awaits us in that concert hall....

After recording my morning entry herein, I dressed at once and began de-cluttering my only means of egress. I had wanted to see about my father's condition. Indeed, it made me anxious in the extreme not doing so, and yet I knew then that we were being watched, and I decided it tantamount that my destination and intentions remained unspoken.

The village was still as a stage set between acts and loaded with a feeling of dreadful imminence. The sun, erumpent only an hour earlier, had become obscured by a roll of ashen clouds so dense it seemed the coming of dusk. I knew I had little time before the rain recommenced, and thus moved swiftly in pursuit of my aims.

My hopes of hiring a coach were frustrated almost immediately; after an extensive search I came upon a livery stable, stocked with carriages but alas no horses. Locating a physician among the mute and shuttered houses and storefronts was equally fruitless, and so I went to the seamstress's shop, which I found also to be closed and locked. Upon her stoop I held out my fist to rap on the door and then paused, for it seemed instinctively unwise to disturb the silence, as if I might wake something marauding and hideous, lying in abeyance only due to lack of sport. I was startled when the door suddenly opened and Miss Saffrey, as if anticipating my arrival, ushered me inside without a word. She shut and re-bolted it, then led me upstairs to a cold and cramped garret.

It was simple and austere, with only the necessary appliances and furnishings for a solitary life. Across from the landing was a coal stove in which no fire burned despite the considerable chill. Under the eave at one end was a bed on which dozed a large and lumpy red cat. Near this was a plain vanity with a diamond-shaped mirror. Purple ribbon, a pile of hair pins, and a brush lay on its surface. There was a washbasin, a chamber pot. At the other end beyond the stairwell and near the other eave was a table and chairs; a single taper in a wrought iron holder stood on the tabletop. A squat cabinet housed teacups and other bone-ware. Modest yet decorative rugs lay upon the pine floorboards. No paintings hung on the plaster walls—the only extravagance I saw was a low shelf packed with slim volumes (poetry mostly, it appeared) at the foot of the bed. Standing there, amongst her few things filled me with an intense envy, for despite its humble trappings it was, unequivocally, a *home*.

She bade me sit at the little table and then went to the window and looked out past the lichen-blanketed slate tiles of the neighboring roof to the street below, her hands clamped together, her expression grim. At length she left the window, wrapped herself in a shawl which was lying over the other chair opposite me and sat. Neither of us spoke, and for a long moment the only sound was the snoring of the cat.

"I regret that I am not able to offer you any tea," Miss Saffrey said finally. "But the fire must not be lit." When I asked why not she replied: "Do you not know the danger you are in, Mr. Layne?"

"That is why I have come, though more for my father's sake."

"You have left him ... *there* ... on his own?"

"I had no choice. He is ill and in urgent need of a physician's care."

"I am sorry to hear it," she said, staring at the pitted wooden surface of the table, "and regret to inform you that you will no longer find any physician here."

I leaned forward. "What happened to him, Miss Saffrey? What is going on in this village? What do you know about the Canis family and about that castle?"

She looked up at me, her brow bent. "You do not see it...."

"No. Please, *help me to*."

A sound reached us then—the puncturing of glass, a clattering noise, and the echo of a shriek. In such propinquity was it to where we sat that for an instant I thought the origin was inside the shop. On the bed the cat hissed. Instinctively I picked up the instrument case as Miss Saffrey rose and went to the window, glancing down at the house below and then drawing the heavy curtain. For a moment all was dark and still; then I heard her soft steps, the rattle of a chatelaine and the sliding of the lid of a match cellar. The strike of phosphorus revealed her trembling hands—trembling to such a degree that she struggled to light the taper. Gently I took it from her and touched flame to wick.

For some time after we sat in waiting silence with the candle glowing between us like a secret. I felt a nudge against my leg, looked down and saw the cat there, slobbering and slack-eyed. It let out a groaning mew and butted the top of its head against my calf, repeating the cycle several times before I reached down and scratched its bristly neck.

"That's Pendleton," Miss Saffrey said. I made the observation that he was quite the old boy, to which she replied while gazing at him with loving poignancy: "Twenty-two. He has been with me always. Come, Pen—that is not yours...."

The cat quit the instrument case upon which he had been rubbing his face and stalked toward her. He let her pick him up and settled on her lap Sphinx-like, recommencing his purring as she stroked him. "He is hungry, poor fellow ... I have not been out in several days...."

It would not occur to me until later that she hadn't a crumb to eat in her pantry. How remorseful I feel now in not offering then my assistance in procuring for her and her companion some means of sustenance....

"I need to tell you about something that happened many years ago," she said. Here she paused, and I waited without comment as she gathered her thoughts. "My mother disappeared when I was fifteen. Like the others, she did not return and nothing of hers was ever discovered. I was however fortunate in some regard, having some notion at least of who was responsible. Someone came to the shop a week prior to her disappearance—a woman neither of us had seen before...."

"Was she from Teethsgate?" I asked.

"It was mid-February and the coldest night yet of a winter miserable with copious bouts of snow and ice. My mother and I were sewing in the rooms below when we heard the knock. It had been casual, without the urgency one would presume from one out in such conditions. I can recall my mother regarding the door for a long time without moving. The knock sounded again—the same light cadence as before. I asked: "Should we answer it?", to which my mother gave no reply. As you may have surmised, being two women on our own in a village of coastal transients—seamen and the like—we were not in the habit of answering calls past dark.

"The knocking, however, went on—without cessation and eerily without increase in exigency. At last my mother rose, crossed to the window and peered through a narrow line between the curtains. She ordered me then to go upstairs and not come down until instructed to. I obeyed, though as soon as I heard the door open, I snuck two steps down and peered below at the figure standing on our stoop. Her cloak and the hair beneath the drawn up hood were the color of lava. Indeed, she was like a blaze before the whiteout, a thing burning from within, oblivious to the cold."

"What did she want?" I said.

"Iron thread—a *spool* of it."

"Forgive me, I'm not familiar …"

"It is the most expensive—and most caustic—weave in the world; a blended strand of shellacked cotton and the web of the Tung spider. The web itself is so strong it has been known to ensnare crows. Long term contact with the skin will result in acute burns. One is advised to wear gloves coated with carbolic acid when handling it."

"If not garments, what is it used for?" I asked.

"Primarily for the protection and display of rare jewels, gems, and precious metals. I understand the royal treasury contains no less than fifty such pieces. The woman paid in full, in bullion no less, ten times the quoted price. My mother accepted, though she was chary of the whole business, for the woman was dubious. But how could one eschew a boon of such magnitude? It was the equivalent of several years' salary. If managed conservatively, this might have sustained our small household for a decade or more…."

"Is this material difficult to acquire?"

"Unadulterated Tung web is found on only a single remote island situated in a notoriously perilous latitude of the lower seas. It is a four-month round-trip journey from which fewer than half the ships that attempt it return. My mother entrusted a third of the ingots with a captain scheduled to pilot a merchant vessel to that region. It departed upon the clearing of the storm, and returned at last as the first daffodil bonnets were opening.

"The red woman was upon our stoop only hours after it arrived, without notice and without being sent for. Again I watched from the stairs as my mother handed her the dutifully wrapped package, warning her once again of the thread's toxicity. To this the woman made no reply. As she was turning to leave, Pendleton, who had crept down beside me, uttered a hungry mew which drew the woman's gaze. When she looked up, her eyes fixed directly on mine. I can recall distinctly that they were—"

"Different colors," I said.

The cat, as if to illustrate his part in the story, suddenly leapt with surprising nimbleness onto the table and then down into my lap where he began rubbing his wet muzzle on my hand. Miss Saffrey, ignoring this act of feline impudence, said with a look of palpable terror: "You've seen her?"

"It is the Countess Canis," I said. "She resides at Teethsgate with the Count and their daughter."

"Canis?" she gasped.

The effect of this name upon her perplexed me, and gave me pause. I asked whether or not they were the undisputed lords of the Westvold, to which Miss Saffrey gave a most unsettling reply.

"I know nothing of the family you have mentioned. The castle itself is ancient. It predates this village by centuries and therefore little is known of its original inhabitants. No one from town ventures there, as wolves abound in the northern woods, though they seldom enter our borders. Several years ago there went about a rumor that a family had taken up residence there. Some men went thither, and when they returned they told of a man in black staring at them from atop the keep, perched there like some giant bird of prey. He was accompanied by a flock of white and black rooks, or so the men said."

"And no one has to your knowledge been there since?"

"None save you," she said darkly.

"When did people begin to vanish?" I asked.

She pondered the question a moment. "If my recollection is

accurate, a few months prior to my mother's disappearance. Over the years, they have decreased in interval, and increased in number."

I considered this while indolently stroking the cat, who was heavy and quite malodorous. I did not mind, however, for the garret was snug with the candle burning between us and the rain lashing the roof and the wind singing its dirge in the eaves. As I regarded the flame, the word *caustic* kept repeating in my mind.

"The necklace!" I ejaculated, so loudly I startled the cat from my lap. "That is what the Countess wanted with the thread. She made a necklace from it for Daeva."

"Who is Daeva?" Miss Saffrey said.

"Their daughter."

"How casually you speak her name," she said.

"She has worn the thing every day since my father and I have been guests at the castle. It is a hideous, sprawling thing encasing a large gemstone," I said, circumventing her allusion, though the sudden color in my countenance most surely had given me away.

Miss Saffrey was shaking her head. "It could not possibly be worn in such a manner. Flesh turns necrotic where it touches."

"I tell you, this is what the iron thread was used for. I am certain of it."

"How is it that you are so certain?" she said. Her eyes drifted to the instrument case and remained there as if it were a dog she feared would strike. "You carry that everywhere, I presume?"

"It is my charge," I replied.

"Perhaps the same could be said for the girl and the gem."

"What are you implying, Miss Saffrey?"

"Evil attracts Evil."

"How careless of you then, inviting one so obviously malevolent into your home," I rejoined.

"Please do not mistake me, Mr. Layne. I am not suggesting that you are *yourself* evil, only being led by an instrument of such attribute."

I asked on what grounds was she basing her deduction, to which she replied:

"I wonder: have you seen yourself perform, sir?"

I rose abruptly, put on my coat and picked up the instrument case. "I appreciate your counsel. But I must now return to my father."

She followed me down the stairs, speaking not until I opened the door.

"You should know about the bars of gold we received in payment for the commission."

"Yes?"

"Once the woman had her thread, they turned to common bricks."

I admit my skin prickled at this revelation; indeed it was an image which increased in terror and import as I tramped through the puddled ruts along the slick cobbled way toward town center. The rain was a blinding torrent, thrashing slate and shingle, window and stone. I drew my coat over my head, tucked the instrument case beneath and ran for the square, hoping to find there some portico or hood under which I might take temporary refuge. Arriving thither, I discovered waiting for me a long black coach drawn by a pair of black stallions. It was exceedingly ornate, with tracery detailing on the skeleton boot and flourishing foot boards and splashers. The gamboge velvet interior, illumined by a phantom globe of swirling light, left little in the way of speculation as to from whence it had come.

I entered reluctantly—though it was a relief to be out of the rain—and was stunned to find none other than the Count seated within. The characteristic air of joviality was absent from his features. In fact, he appeared quite vexed. He said nothing in greeting as the door was shut and the wheels began moving. In almost no time we had left Larmes Harbor and were ascending the cliff road up which we surmounted at an immense speed.

"We are most distressed by your insistence on frequently leaving the castle, Maestro," the Count began. "The village is not safe, and its denizens have suffered much. What if you were to disappear like the others? How should we then fare, censured by our contemporaries as the hosts who allowed the world's greatest violist to be abducted from under their very own roof?"

"It was not my intention to trouble you, my lord," I said. "I went only in the interest of my father, who in addition to his croup has been afflicted with an acute inflammation of the leg. I fear that the physician's diagnosis will be grave."

"Alas, you should have consulted with me first! Your father could already be receiving treatment. A member of the Duke's entourage is one of the most skilled practitioners on the continent."

I admitted that I had been unaware of this.

"Indeed, he is," the Count reiterated. "Despite our remoteness, we are rather well connected. This is but a small paradigm of the appurtenances and luxuries you and your father might enjoy should you decide to remain with us."

I frowned. "*Remain* with you?"

"Daeva is much infatuated with you, though I gather that this has already been made evident," the Count said. I felt flames in my cheeks as I looked away, shamed and mortified as I was by his inexplicable knowledge of the previous night's events. He was swift, however, in reassuring me that neither he nor the Countess was dishonored by my actions. On the contrary, he added rather pragmatically: "If you have spoken to the lady and indeed intend to marry, I should like to expedite the union by preëmptively granting my consent. You would become joint heirs, and upon the deaths of myself and the Countess inherit Teethsgate and together rule the Westvold."

I was too bewildered by this to form a reply. Faster we climbed, the coach rocking and bouncing at times with such violence that I had to hold my arms out and press my palms against the sides of the cabin to keep from being tossed about. There was a spectral aspect to the shrill whinnies and guttural groans of the horses as they charged through the rain and shredded mist with increasing speed. A blast of lightning tore a rent in the fabric of fog, and by that ragged and transitory illumination I saw to my utter incredulity the façade of Teethsgate looming in the coach's window. The passage which took at least a half hour we had traversed in less than five minutes.

"I will leave you off here," said the Count. "Go and discuss my proposal with your father. You and he are both our guests for as long as it pleases you. I look forward to this evening's performance most eagerly, as well as your decision."

I exited the coach unsteadily, taking a few steps toward the marble stair where I paused to peer up through the drizzle at the lancet glowing like firelight. I thought: did I leave a candle burning? Behind me the carriage started off in the direction of the rear of the castle. Through bleary eyes, I watched as it disappeared around the corner. I record this here only because I saw no coachman upon the perch; which is to say that the carriage which had carried us hither had made the passage from the village *without anyone guiding it*.

The castle was unexpectedly chill and damp and conspicuously vacant despite the throng of guests I had observed the previous night. I pictured them put away like dolls in one of the rooms or stacked in piles or standing submissively in eerie queues. When I reached the second level I saw that rows of pillar candles had been placed along either side of the passageway leading to my chamber. They were red, as was their light, which conspired with the dark to create cloister-esque shadow arches and gave the walls the appearance of having been brushed with blood. The candles ended at my door, where hung a single red dahlia. From its stem dangled the necklace of Lover's Tongue leaves which Daeva had put around my neck in the garden, now snapped. Looking closely, I noticed that the wilting flower had been *nailed* to the door, and from it the strand of leaves were placed so that it appeared to run like drops of blood.

I did not doubt whom I would find within.

Daeva lay in the bed, disheveled as when I had left her the previous night. The room was exceptionally hot, and upon that heat I could smell her—a luring, conflicting scent which I struggled mind and body in not yielding to. As she sat up the transparent silk shifted, lasciviously exposing her as well as the necklace. I traced its sinewy pattern with my eyes—the thing looked *embroidered* into her flesh! Beyond the bed my trunk lay open, its contents blatantly probed scattered on the floor.

"Hello, my love," she said. Her voice was snow-soft and twice as cold.

I regarded her silently for some time, considering with great care my reply. "I owe you an apology," I said at last. Daeva cocked her head slightly, her expression unchanged. "I behaved in an ungentlemanly manner last night. I hope you will forgive my licentious conduct."

"Why did you go to the village again?" she asked.

My reply was the same as it had been to the Count: that my father's condition has worsened significantly and that I had attempted to locate a physician. As I spoke I eyed the fluctuating lights, whereby I saw something pinched between her fingers like a spider she had plucked from her skirts. It was the scrap of paper from my pocket, the one with Miss Saffrey's warning written upon it. Instinctively, I clasped the instrument case to my chest.

"'Loyalty'—the first of your 'three tenets' as I recall. You would do better in calling it 'Betrayal.'"

I asked whether she made a habit of violating the trust of her guests.

"You are a liar as well as a fraud, Jonas—your purported virtue a mask, same as your virtuosity. And I gave you *everything*," Daeva hissed. Her eyes began to shine, solid and flat gold like an animal's reflected at night. The orbs in the room began to swell and dim sporadically. With each draw the gem brightened, then darkened again, like bellows blowing upon on a fire.

"You speak of 'masks'," I rejoined. "What of your façades, Daeva? What horrors do you here propagate, and at whose expense?"

Her grin was grey in the low light. "I told you that we are the same. Our burdens bind us. Do you think anyone else will have you, knowing your secret? You think *she* will?" Daeva said, waggling the note and then flicking it in my direction. The gemstone was brightening like the opening eye of a waking dragon, and as it grew in luminosity so did a sensation of black seeping into me through the oblong box held to my chest, like hideous fluids leeching through wood and oiled hide into my flesh. I was filled with a radiating cold, the constraining chill of deep soil, and I could not be sure whether the room was darkening or my vision was being occluded by shadow. Still there was the gem light, like the chromosphere around a lunar eclipse, receding as I was suddenly impelled backward through the doorway. The door was drawn shut after me, the gust it created disproportionately powerful and I was thrown against the wall, my breath stopped as the candles went out in a cascade of extinguished wicks, leaving me gasping in the dark.

How long I lay there I cannot say, though I know it was the growl that got me moving.

Crouching, sensorially groping in the blackness, I started to creep along the wall in the direction I hoped was the corridor leading to the stairs. At length I found a corner and was rounding it when I again heard the growl—this time inches from my face. I envisioned the beast standing before me with strands of pearlescent drool dangling from its gaping mouth. It sniffed cursorily, and then padded off down the hall where distantly I heard (and smelled) the bitter reek of urine striking stone. Next came a yowl and scratching at the door—the door to my chamber, or so I reckoned as it was the nearest in proximity. Engaged as it seemed in its plea for admittance, I made haste silently toward the end of the corridor and at last reached the doorway to the stairs.

The interior night, however, did not end there. So black was the stair hall that I found myself questioning whether or not my sight had been stolen. Clinging to the balustrade, I stepped onto the landing, my footfalls amplified conspicuously in the vastness. It took several minutes to reach the bottom, and several more to cross the ocean of stone floor and locate the passage which led to the library.

I half expected the lights to be out there as well, but they were not. My father, to my surprise, was up and already dressed in his concert suit; the obligatory tailcoat and knee breeches, linen shirt with frills and crimson cravat. All at once this attire appeared quaint, antediluvian even. His silk hose ended at one polished and buckled shoe and one bandaged foot. His weedy hair was combed back, his beard trimmed. His waxy countenance was still and impassive, though I saw wistfulness in his rust-colored eyes. On the table beside him stood the bottle of port given to him by the king a decade earlier, and two glasses. It had been all these years like a talisman; he had vowed never to open it as long as we were traveling. Now, the seal was cracked, and it appeared that he had already sampled some himself. He gestured to the chair on the other side of the table and I sat.

"Why have you opened it?" I said, gesturing at the bottle.

"Because it is our last performance," my father said.

So astonished was I by this unexpected assertion I could not speak.

"You want to go home...." he added.

Despite this being the truth I was hesitant in confirming it, for the finality of such an affirmation was more profound in uttering than I had anticipated. And yet the words were there, indeed they had been for some time, and I was ready to utter them. "Yes, Father."

The old man nodded, smiled briefly, then filled the two glasses and raised his in toast. "To you, my son." He swirled, sniffed, and sipped the wine, closing his eyes then opening them again as he savored it. "Mmm. *Perfection.*" He considered the reddish-amber liquid a moment and then softly laughed. "It is the province of the diseased mind, is it not? What folly it is, the quest to attain Genius. Only when we are inevitably ruined from our seeking do we understand such superior aptitude is an accident, maddeningly random and in most cases, *entirely undeserved.*"

I took a slow drink, attempting to divine the projected course of his thoughts. His ruminations often turn discursive—acutely so when imbibing spirits or wine.

"You were right, Jonas. I have been running from your mother's death all these years and have dragged you along with me. I was aggrieved, true, but I was also ambitious—for myself as well as for you. I brought it home to you, and opened the case. It was I who put that viola in your hands. *I* was the one who insisted on greatness, on *perfection*. But you already were. You always have been!"

He was weeping, most gratuitously, I thought. Such an appending seems indeed cruel, but I find my stock of sympathy presently wanting, particularly for confessions made futile by dilatory pronouncement.

"You did not put it in my hands, Father," I said. "I took it, remember?"

To this he made no reply. His concentration was beset with the task of composing himself, which at length he did. When next he spoke it was with the very Theodore-like tenor of practicality. "We've honored every contract, every commitment to the letter all these years. I consent in allowing you to steer our ship upon whatever course you see fit from this night on, so long as you fulfill one final wish: *We play the concert.*"

"Yes, Father. We will play," I said, and, glancing then at the oblong box at my feet, thought: *And then I will destroy it.*

Now, on the eve of this momentous and decidedly obfuscated dénouement, one might suppose that as I sit here with quill in hand my meditations and apprehensions would be centered upon what is imminent, though they are not. What I find myself contemplating is Miss Saffrey's cozy garret, lit by that single taper. The light is a feeble torch in the fuliginous room, where she sits alone with a cup of cold tea, her stinky old mouser on her lap or curled upon her quilt. I see the empty chair across from her, and I wonder whether she pines for it to be occupied once more. It is of course presumptuous and audacious to postulate her feelings. I know that I long to again be seated there, and yet I possess neither the respectability nor composure requisite of such esteemed company. Isadora Saffrey is a penurious spinster, and will be for the rest of her days most likely. Her life stretches before her like a barren winter plain, nonetheless she will cross it with self-possession and honor.

Evil attracts Evil, she said to me. As I now look upon the viola I see—I *feel*—that it is an extension of me; a continuation of my being, like an appendage of sinew and bone. To destroy it would be as well my ruin.

Our burdens bind us....

Daeva, it seems, was equally as veracious in her estimation.

12th April, 1800
Larmes Harbor

For several months, since their discovery in the pile upon the hill, these pages have lain untouched. Until presently I had been hesitant in reading them for fear of redoubling the Horror which I have only recently begun to assess with any semblance of rationality and reason. I did so at last with the hope that such a revisiting might aid in bringing to an end the night terrors. Closure I did *not* seek, for some wounds never close.

And so I took up the MS with a prior resolution of burning it after perusal—as an act of symbolic liberation from the Past if nothing more. Having done so, I have however delayed in carrying out its obliteration, due mostly to its haunting *in praesenti* recounting of my father and those harrowing hours at Teethsgate Castle, though also for its merit as an instruction on the consequences of vanity, should I ever need reminding.

It is now Spring, and with the advent of the new season, I have decided it right to append these stained and rumpled pages with the remainder of the tale; to conclude, as it were, one life before beginning another....

Every candle in the mirrored foyer was lit, so that the space sparkled with the infinity of a star-scattered sky. The doors to the concert hall were open, and beyond I heard the hum of hundreds of ardent voices. With my father on my arm, we entered and were instantly met with an eruption of applause as well as a rush of distracting light—the glimmer of thousands of diamond-bright reflections and refractions off the bejeweled courtiers and the honed facets of the crystal chandeliers. It was the most decadent and decidedly eccentric assemblage I had ever beheld, and every seat in the hall was filled, even those in the upper gallery. The throng filling them was garbed anachronistically and bizarrely in apparent costume, though the mood was unequivocally formal and without a trace of the flippancy or irreverence typical of a *bal masqué*.

For a moment we could do nothing more than stand there with

surprise writ across our faces. I for one had anticipated a more perilous welcome, and I located at once the vengeful girl, who wore a gown the same shade as the crucified dahlia on my door and was seated to the left of her mother beside the Duke. Her glare, and that of Danesfall's, was of uniform malignity, suggesting that he had been made privy to my rebuffing of his cousin. The Count rose then, tamping down the strident approbation by gesturing briefly with both palms pressed forward for the crowd to be seated.

"My dear friends," he began, "the Countess and I welcome you to our home on this rare and illustrious occasion. Tonight we will hear the debut performance of a new sonata entitled 'The Three Tenets of Love', whose creator is no other than the *Maestro célèbre* Jonas Layne, the world's greatest violist!" A spirited ovation followed. "He is accompanied, as always, by his father and pedagogue, Mr. Theodore Layne." Another round of ovation as my father bowed. "It has been both an honor and a pleasure to have these gentlemen as our guests this last week. Alas, this concert is the culmination of their time here at Teethsgate, though our regret is assuaged at the knowledge that a part of them shall *always* remain within these walls."

I recall these words with an insoluble chill, for there had been no disclosure to the Count of our definite plans of departure. Furthermore, as he spoke he had turned and looked back at me *with eyes that did not seem his own.*

I guided my father to the brief set of stairs leading to the stage, which he ascended bravely and, almost inconceivably, without any audible protestations of pain, and then toward the piano where he was seated. I crossed to the table opposite the grand, unpacked the viola and carried it to the front of the stage where I announced the names of the three movements. As silence established dominion in the hall, the lights of the chandeliers and the vertical and cylindrical vessels along the walls dimmed like the sun beclouded. I held the viola to my neck, felt it *lock* more fixedly than I had ever before. I raised the bow and brought it down.

Sound bellowed from the Inamorta, a death-moan filling the cavity of the hall: three slow draws of the band of rosined hair across the low C followed by a furious solo in presto time, the intonation flawless. On my left I heard my father pounding out the marching harmony, adding flourishes of notes which punctuated each passage in counterpoint. Not halfway through the piece, the viola began to vibrate with violent force; these vibrations ran down my bowing arm, initially only a tickle, though rapidly intensifying into a maddening itch, and finally a tattoo of piercing pain, each note like a thorn prick. I attempted to cease playing but found to my horror that I could not. An excruciating pressure mounted in my skull. I could not determine whether it would implode or explode, though one or the other was certainly imminent. Meanwhile my hands flew up and down the fingerboard at a preternatural pace, producing music which was no longer music as such, but rather an acrimonious wail.

I stumbled, my mouth filled with a burning metallic taste. With great effort I opened my eyes and saw at first only the gemstone, blazing like blood filtered sunlight beneath Daeva's crimson gown. Then a black arm rose up from the Inamorta's bass-side f-hole and anchored itself palm-down on the arched top of the instrument. A figure pushed upward, toward me—an encroaching wall of shadow eclipsing all as I pitched forward blindly, still playing, into the empty orchestra pit.

Giovanni's Tale

*I*t was dusk, and the windows of the shelter cut into the mountain glowed like cats' eyes. The cauldron had shown him the place, as it had everything else: the tree, the field hand, the very plan itself. It had been an uninhabitable shell, requiring weeks of repair and restoration before the work could begin there. Unlike the home atelier, this was a simple place, deliberately austere and intentionally far from the distraction (and suspicion) of the city, for paramount it was that this work was unseen and uninterrupted.

Within, the great maker sat hunched at a crude table which had become his de facto bench, the ridges of his spine tenting his filthy shirt, his hair hanging like shredded curtains framing his sallow, prematurely lined face. His eyes were fixed upon the unvarnished yew viola lying before him. It had taken six months to craft, and in that span—the same during which the voice had haunted his house—envy and obsession had transformed the once-celebrated master luthier of Cremorta into a monomaniacal ghoul. Though he was cognizant of this, it mattered nothing to him. This was the sacrifice necessary in order for him to forge his magnum opus, the instrument which would redeem him and carry his name banner-like through the ages. It had not been "made" like his other instruments, but forged in the scorched chambers of his blackened, indurate heart. This viola would be both his vehemence and vengeance incarnate, formed in her image and binding immortally to wood that tormenting voce infernale, *subjugate forever after.*

He had first heard it during a night walk near the woods south of the city perimeter. The moon illumined the meadow and hills, but its pale eye did not penetrate the copse from whence came the voice like a myth, drawing him near though not beyond the barrier of trees. The black was too absolute, and the source of the mellifluous and incorporeal alto uncertain. Its transcendent singularity remained with him, however; the phantom dirge possessed his thoughts so entirely that for several nights thereafter he wandered the surrounding locality to no avail in search of its owner. Though Morturia was not an irrational man, he nonetheless found himself contemplating whether or not it had truly been wraith song, for what chanteuse of such dutiful training and refined inflection would be roving scrub and country?

He heard it next most unexpectedly while traversing the ring road within the Cremortan boundary. So faint was it he had thought it in his head though soon he recognized it as a variation of that original melody scratched upon the staves of his memory. Rushing toward the city gates, he ordered the guards to throw open the doors and out he ran, pausing only to allow his ear a moment to ascertain the direction of the voice. He tracked it to a low and secluded bank of the river where, squatting at the water's edge with her feet sunk in the mud, was a scraggy girl of perhaps eighteen dressed in scarecrow rags. She dragged her fingers back through her black hair as she sang, the long bands lifting and falling like the dark wings of a nycticorax. And as he listened, weeping without shame or self-censure at its beauty and purity, he thought: it exists. That which he had sought to produce for thirty years in each one of his instruments was here, embodied within this frail vessel—alas, the wrong vessel, bound to flesh as it was. So he had captured the filthy rube and had done her the supreme honor of making her his wife.

This he had later regretted. In addition to being coarse and laconic, she had not been a virgin. It was to some measure inconsequential to Morturia, as he had not apprehended her for the purpose of fornication (though indeed enjoying the pleasure at one's leisure was the privilege of owning one's wife), but to study her, or rather her remarkable faculty.

What had occurred instead was the improbable usurpation of his techne. With half a year vanished, not only were his three attempts at replicating that haunting timbre splinters in the rubbish, equally in shambles were his impetus and ego, for the voice had become a curse. It seemed to mock him contemptuously; even to hear her speak was anathema. He loathed the very sight of her, and though it was his own edict which decreed that she remain within the palazzo, so extreme was his jealously that he would not, despite himself, release her into the city.

And so he abandoned his atelier, where he had labored a quarter of a century crafting instruments which would sing centuries beyond his death. The fastidious gentleman luthier became disheveled and was often drunk. He ceased working, released his apprentices and the servants, and took to wandering to remote terrains which he had never traversed— regions of lore in the penumbra of the mountains. In these shunned wilds he wandered like a tramp, even sleeping there on occasion rather than return to the house where slept the voice. Once such place was a mephitic marsh formed from an ancient lake from which shadows were said to rise like stands of cypress. Giovanni saw these during one of his treks, hideous flame-shaped things they were, portents perhaps of his later discovery that same day of the shelter and the cauldron.

The ancient stone domicile he had glimpsed first, partially set within and protruding from an outcrop on a rise overlooking the bog. Though ownerless and scattered with old bones it stank of wounds. From one crudely hewn window he surveyed the lowlands. Looking down through the strata of fog and shadow he saw rising from the fens a grey and massive yew, lined and sinewy as an old throat. Its bare limbs, like frozen lightning, bore no needles, nor blood-red berries.

He descended to it, and almost at once saw dull silver peering through the hulking, half-exposed roots. The wood there was soft, and the spongy tentacles ceded the cauldron with little resistance. The latter was immensely heavy; it took nearly an hour for him to drag it back up the hillside to the shelter where after a breathless respite he examined the burden in question. It was indeed silver—solid throughout. Cast in low relief along its breadth were wordless scenes graphically depicting abduction and sacrifice. A bound figure was being led to a clearing. In the next panel it was screaming as its limbs were severed and then offered piece by piece to the cauldron. In the third, the figure rose out transformed, the eyes and mouth gaping caverns.

Morturia touched lightly these images, considering them. The metal warmed and pulsated pleasantly beneath his fingers. He looked inside and saw it filled with water. How was it so? He had emptied it surely before carrying it hither. He tipped it on its side but the liquid would not pour out, rather it receded against the walls and pooled under the inner lip. Righted once again, the water returned to the center of the basin where it remained, half filling the vessel. He submerged his hand in it. Indeed it felt like water, tepid and innocuous. The surface however did not ripple and when he drew the hand out it was not wet.

Intrigued, he commenced a series of experiments. He added more water; it beaded like glass upon the surface and ran out onto the floor when he upended the cauldron. He put in dead leaves, twigs, a stone. It smoked; the surface simmered slightly, then went again still. The objects, however, did not come back out. He threw in a dead fly, a snail shell, a handful of dirt. More smoke; nothing else. He snatched a fat spider crawling across the floor and fed it to the silver pot. This time the smoke was rust orange, and the surface acquired a dull sheen like tarnished glass. There upon an image began to resolve, though nothing solidifying beyond a myopic blur of colors.

He smacked the side once, then three times violently, cutting his hand on a point jutting from one of the carvings. As he held it up, grimacing, blood dripped into the opening. Black smoke boiled red, and with mirror clarity a vision sharpened and blazed.

His wife was standing on the little balcony outside her room in a flowing crimson dress. She was singing to a crowd gathered below which was gazing up at her in dazed adoration. Who was this woman? Why have we not seen her? Why has this treasure been kept from us, and who is responsible? Their reproving eyes looked to him, and then she turned, her glare equally as reproachful as that sardonic voice poured from her. In the next moment the image began to blur, the color fading like that of flowers in frost, and then it vanished.

Morturia banged the side again, the cauldron clanging like a bell as he struck it, bringing new blood. He paused, regarding it, then held his fist over the opening and squeezed. The scene returned at once, spreading along the surface as the blood diffused there. This time he saw the ancient yew in the clearing. He saw himself approaching it with a great axe with which he used to fell the organic pillar and cleave it to its heartwood. He then carried a section of this back to the shelter which was set up like his atelier.

The vision began to dissolve. He raised his hand, offered more of himself. He did this several times, and when ere long all was revealed, he dragged the cauldron to the corner of the room, covered it with brush, and returned post hence to the palazzo.

A fortnight on, he sat with a pair of book-matched yew panels which, when held together there formed down the middle the dark image of a cloaked figure with a hood like a candle snuff. Morturia grinned, his teeth a pale shade of rust in the tallow light. He joined the pieces with hide glue and then, scrapping all forms, patterns, and measurements, completed the instrument over the subsequent month solely on intuition. It was a ghastly thing to behold; the sum of its detail rendering it more the coffin of a monster than instrument: that blood pool grain pattern, those corners like gargoyle wingtips, the clenched skeletal hand atop the neck. When it was finished, he snipped a small rectangle of parchment, and taking up his pen, wrote in careful script:

"The Inamorta"
per mano di
Giovanni Morturia, Cremorta, 1589
– Death's Beloved ... May He Hold Thee Eternal –

He brushed this with glue, slid it through an f-hole and pasted it to the back of the viola. Then he made the long journey through the woods back to the home atelier, where he would wait.

When he left Cremorta again it was at gloaming. He was wearing the young man's clothes and pushing a loaded cart, its cargo covered with rags. From the city gates to the shelter was a three hour trek over morass and root and stones; arriving thither he wanted only sleep, but there was no margin for hesitation.

The viola lay on its back on his bench, a cord tied around the grasping scroll. He unloaded the cart, placing the lidded jar beside the cauldron on his bench, and the whore on the table he had constructed for this moment. She did not stir from her ether induced sleep as he unbound her limbs and retied them using the same rope to iron rings jutting up from the wooden surface. He wrapped a strip of black canvas around her mouth, and another band around her chin, tying these in a way which caused her head to tilt back and her throat to arch.

He removed the lid from the jar and emptied the young man's genitals into a shallow bowl, then took up his purfling knife and went back to where the whore lay. The skin paste made of crushed egg shell which she applied to nullify her peasant bronze was blotched and smeared, and her splayed hair was so black it was like a scorch stain upon the table. She was waking. She bucked against the circulation-stopping knots. He grinned, watching the terrors accrete in her eyes. She made only the smallest sound; the Voice was gagged. His grin became a rictus. She was meanwhile frantic. Her eyes ran like fountains as they focused on the blade moving toward her.

Morturia inserted it, first on one side of the throat, then the other, with the same slow and careful precision as he did when slicing through soft spruce. Spurts of blood shot geyser-like from the wounds, striking the ceiling, and he leapt back in shock. Foolishly he had put a bucket below the table as a basin for the blood, but this wasn't like the young man dangling from the makeshift atelier gallows—this was a living, fighting human body, the heart pounding triple time, ejaculating blood everywhere. He waited; let her lie jerking and quivering as the flow reduced to a bubble and finally a trickle. Rapidly she perished, slathered in her own life fluid, and when it was over, he sliced through the muscle and sinew, cartilage and the disks of fluid and nerve (though careful not to damage the throat) then carried the head by the hair and set it upright on the table beside the bowl.

He removed the bandage from his wrist and opened the old cut with the purfling knife. His own blood simmered in the cauldron like a pot just before boiling. Next went in the contents of the shallow bowl, turning the "water" a swampy green. He picked up the whore's head by the hair and slowly submerged it, then threw in the knife. The cauldron frothed, a noxious stew of viscera color and smell. Black smoke billowed upward, cycling back to its source and each time it reëmerged it was in the form of some hideous elaboration of violence. To watch this resorbing and wicked unfurling was to become devitalized perpetually by new grief, and through several cycles Morturia could do nothing but regard the horrors with the irreducible awe of one buried alive. The moment, however, was passing; ere long the opportunity would be squandered, and it was his innate need for retribution and self-preservation which propelled him to action.

Snatching the raw viola, he held it by the cord looped around the scroll, and standing over the boiling maelstrom, began to lower it in. The cauldron was not deep enough to admit the instrument entirely, and yet the latter sank nonetheless, down to the tips of his knuckles. The smoke quit its outward roiling and plunged down after it like a horde of starving rats. There was a tremendous thunder, like a boulder rolling down the mountain toward the shelter, followed by a single slashing scream—then stillness.

Morturia withdrew the instrument. The cauldron hissed and sighed as if satisfied. He looked inside and saw that it was once again, except for the "water," uncannily empty. The viola was char-black, with an inky luster which appeared to undulate subtly with the sheen of the sea under a full moon. He turned it in his hands, marveling at the uniform ebony contours. The grain lines were shadowed furrows, and the only variation in shade was the hooded figure running vertically and symmetrically down the seam where the two plates of the instrument's back joined. This was the shade of venous blood. The color brightened somewhat beneath his fingers, drawing, or so it seemed to, warmth from his touch while the rest of the body remained cold as the walls of a winter tomb. He tilted the viola horizontally under the candlelight and looked through the treble-side f-hole. Nothing happened for several seconds, then: movement—the blink of black eyes—and he saw that he was once again Master.

He cut bone from the headless corpse, then tossed the body, the cauldron, and everything else that would fit into the cart and wheeled it down to the marsh where with a single thrust, he pushed into the mire. He remained for the three-quarters of an hour it took to fully sink, then returned to the shelter. He placed the viola in an oblong case built specially for it and started back toward Cremorta.

That same night at the home atelier, he added a fingerboard and tuning pegs and carved a bridge, tailpiece, and nut. He rounded and polished the fragments of bone and used them as ornamentation on the button and the ears of the scroll. Lastly, he wound gut strings through the tailpiece and into the peg box, and with a shudder of both dread and enchanted glee, watched them one by one—C,G,D,A—tune without his aid to the correct pitch.

Morturia stood, picked up the viola and a bow. He raised it, hesitated, then lowered it and carried it instead up to her room. The doors leading to the balcony were open. The midnight wind tousling the translucent curtains was laden with voices and scents: inebriated laughter; decadent profumo; the distant hint of harvested wheat.

Below passed the affluent throng, engrossed in their whimsies and dalliances. Standing aloft on this small stage, he would stun them, shake them from their preponderant fancies and make them tremble and weep. He held the viola to his neck, startled by the way in which it suctioned to him. He raised the bow; the hair was taut and well-rosined. Morturia was but an amateur player at best. If the transformation had been achieved with accuracy, skill would matter little.

The bow bit string but made no sound. He glanced down at it, a frown replacing his triumphant grin. He bore down upon the C—nothing—then randomly across all the strings. He paused, assessed the rosin, made several more passes which produced only silence. Some of the passers-by below had *noticed. They stared upward, perplexed. They whispered, they chortled at the mad luthier with his mute instrument. Through this he sawed on, the hair snapping at tip and frog and flailing about. Then, rising, a breath— expanding to a low growl, and then an ear-throttling bellow. It poured, Vesuvian-like, from the viola, soaring through the air and down every street and alley, ricocheting off the walls and barriers. It spiderwebbed window panes and made the bells in the towers hum atonally.*

The citizenry fell to its knees, palms pressed to the sides of their heads, their skulls filled with the thunder of avalanche. On the little balcony, Morturia's brain vibrated to jelly in its case and leaked out through his nose and down the back of his throat. His eyes burst from their sockets and dangled by their optical strands against his cheeks. Still he played, a string-less marionette performing a corybantic danse macabre, and when the sound stopped he was pitched forward, a senseless weight of bone and meat and blood-dappled flesh thrown over the rail and down onto the cobbles. The Inamorta fell too, striking the uneven stones with a resounding clatter as its single pernicious note reverberated like ripples on the sea after a tsunami.

One by one in the city of Cremorta, they unclamped their tremulous hands. They rose, encircled the contorted wreckage of the great maker. None, however, would approach his last capolavoro. The unblemished instrument lay where it had fallen like some alien vessel, shunned for the entirety of the soundless night and the mist-occluded morning which followed. It was Morturia's solicitor who, after shuttering the palazzo and securing the estate, retrieved it, using a silk cloth to lift it from the street and place it inside the oblong box, which he hastily closed. The latter traveled to his ufficio, then via carriage to the damp, grim, and predominantly vacant Schloss von Glahn where for eleven years it remained locked in a Kunstkabinett in an otherwise empty room.

Coiled in the wooden belly, she stared up at the vaulted darkness where never moon nor star appeared to adorn her eternal night. Deprived of crescent and chiaroscuro, madness became her country, and over that blind terrain she set her songs to flight, sable wings rising and diving over pitch plain. Despite this living entombment, she did not despair, for she knew that one day fingers would work the case's latches. The lid would open, and she would gaze up through those notched and angled slits at the new Master. He would lift her out, slide his fingers along her contours, guide her into the warm crook of his neck. She would fasten herself to him—an unrelenting hold—and as he played and she sang, his vitality would flow into her, an inexorable drip-drain, and for a short time, she would be quenched; yes, she would be satisfied.

Though never avenged.

The Chamber of Clive Ravis

I awoke on my back on a bed reeking of mildew in a room that I did not recognize. Across from where I lay a fire burned in the shallow cavity of a black manteled fireplace. The alternating lick of light and shadow was garish and frightful to me in my state of disorientation. I attempted to rise, and felt at once the muscles in my left shoulder and neck seize, followed by a rushing throb at the back of my head on the opposite side. I raised my hand to it, and found a concentration of gauze there, held in place with a length of bandage wrapped about my head. A line of blood had seeped from underneath, run down my cheek, and dried to a crust.

I managed to push myself up onto my elbows and forearms, and then against the headboard where for several minutes I stared stupidly at the flames. Something of dreadful import had occurred: of that there was no doubt, though I could not recall precisely what. It was the ebon scorches on the fireplace walls that triggered the memories of the concert (the black hand, the sun-bright gem), and in the next instant I was overcome by a nauseating certainty.

She has it.

The realization made the pain irrelevant. I turned in the bed, attempted to thrust myself off and in the process nearly swooned. I slid back against the wall, where I rested for several minutes with my eyes closed. When I again opened them I saw across from me a massive desk, piled precariously with books and stacks of parchment. There was an inkwell and pot of black quills and stumps of tallow tapers on wrought-iron prickets. Though I did not see one, I knew that a chamber pot was in the vicinity. Above the desk hung an oil painting of a woman in a smoke-stained frame. The portrait was in profile, which aided in accentuating greatly the aquiline nose. The face was turnip white, the hair and eyes glossy black like the necklace she wore: a blue-black stone set in a claw-like clasp. I saw in my periphery another white face—a bust, or so I presumed—of similar countenance, which I did not give especial notice to until I saw it blink.

A man was seated beside the desk. I recognized him immediately, despite having seen him only twice, briefly, and when he had appeared incorporeal. His antiquated black suit was the same shade as the tarry shadows, rendering him visually almost inextricable from them. The stone hanging from the leather cord about his neck, the same as that in the portrait, had an esoteric, oily luster, as if it were a third eye regarding me.

I asked: what is this place, and who are you? He replied, in a voice that was croaking and indeed corporeal: "Blackspeak Castle. I am the Caretaker."

"Why have we left Teethsgate? Where is my father?"

"You have not, as it were, left the palace of illusions," he replied.

"Are you under the employ of Count Canis?" I inquired.

The man laughed; a gravelly drag that I hoped not to hear repeated. "This is my ancestral home. The House of *Ravis*. My name is Clive Ravis, last of the line of the magus Rooks."

His pupil-less gaze was alight with the thrill of revelation, though for my part all that was revealed was that without question *this man was insane*. And then I recalled the warnings of the Count and the Countess concerning a man in black, and Miss Saffrey's tale of the men from Larmes Harbor who ventured hither and what they had seen perched atop the towers. My stomach began to churn as if filled with warm yarn.

"Where is my father?" I repeated.

"Men like yourself purposely renounce modesty and truth, do they not, Mr. Layne? Humility and self-denial are affronts to their dignity. They are drawn to pomp and pageantry like rats to poisoned bait, oblivious or worse—unconcerned with the consequences of partaking in such sordid enticement. I have watched you the last several days sauntering alongside the thief—consorting with her, committing improprieties with her. *Aye,* you are indeed equally louche as she."

Ignoring the slight, I said: "You are referring to the girl, Daeva, I presume."

"I know not the ghoul's name, if she in fact has one. I do know, with absolute certainty, that she is no 'girl.'"

"What is she then? You call her a ghoul, a thief. How is this reckoned?"

The Caretaker paused, considering the question, then said: "Presently, you see this room as it is, in its state of decrepitude, yes?"

I observed the setting with care and scrutiny, and nodded when I had concluded.

"Good. Then we are seeing things *as they are,* unaltered by my ancestor's wicked enchantments."

At this, a praenomen suddenly entered my mind—one which without hesitation I pronounced. "Rainer?"

For the first time the man's countenance betrayed its mask-like stolidity. There was surprise and fearful reverence in his expression. "Where did you hear of that name?"

"From your own lips, as you knelt before him," I said. My gaze shifted to the stone, that third eye, set in one of two orbital socket-like openings in the silver pendant hanging around his neck.

Ravis' stare hardened. "No, you could not have witnessed this— you could not have followed me thither...."

"Witness it I did," I said. "I saw you remove the necklace from his bound corpse. And now I begin to understand why you call her thief. What she has ... you seek to reclaim it, do you not?"

"The gem is my charge, my burden. '*Pawuk-crix Roak Aerex,*'— 'Keepers of the Cold Flame.' This is the motto of the Rook," the Caretaker croaked.

"How does it work?"

"It has the ability to draw the life-energy from its victim, and repurpose it to whatever aim he chooses; a means of concealment, or perhaps a burst of force. *How* it works—that is known, as its maker intended, only to its possessor, though I surmise that as it gives to its owner, it simultaneously empties him. Rainer apprenticed with the clan's elders, and from them inherited a singular gemstone, which he imbued with incantations. He was obsessed with animism, you see, and for years labored at extracting bodies of sentient energy from seemingly insentient sources such as rock, water, bark—all to no avail. He tried baubles and clothing once owned and worn by the dead, even coffins and mud from the grave, but was thwarted as well in these. At length he moved beyond inert objects and began experimenting with animals. He discovered that he could remove provisionally the soul of a crow and replace it with his own. This was how he and his brothers came to this land, from across the sea in the form of—"

"—black carrion birds ..." I said, meeting his gaze. "*You* placed that book in the library. We thought it a fairy tale."

"It is biography," he replied, "the story of my ancestor's alchemy and how it led to the dismantling of his House. Alas, in the years since the only flame I have preserved is that of the chronicle of a nearly extinct line."

Of course I took this to be apocryphal. His isolation there, I conjectured, had caused his madness—or perhaps the reverse. I looked at the desk with its piles of pages, scrolls, tomes and wondered: Did all of these as well contain his fictions?

"This alchemy was the reason he was bound and walled up in the crypt?" I asked.

"There is nothing we hide so well as dark history," the Caretaker said. "Indeed he was shackled there by his own brethren. What doomed him was the subsequent shifting of his métier from replacement and transformation to that of *acquisition*. People began to vanish from the village. There were whispers of accusation by the villagers, and ere long the men organized, seeking to move on the castle with the aim of usurpation. The brothers would not lose their territorial foothold solely because of Rainer's avarice, and so in clan solidarity they acted, preëmptively and against one of their own."

I added: "And now people are disappearing again...."

"Keeping illusions intact is not without a cost," said Ravis. "The soul is finite as the body, merely *information*. It burns—sun-hot and ice-dry—though the arc of its blaze is unstable and transient. Soon it cools, fades, becomes transparent; its veiling ability degenerates until it is nothing at all. I believe the thief has near exhausted the gem's stores, those begun by Rainer himself. That is why she lured you. She had learned, perhaps by rumor, that you possessed something extraordinary. An object of *in*exhaustible, indivisible, *endless* utility. You do indeed possess such an object, don't you Mr. Layne?"

"Who is she, Mr. Ravis?"

The Caretaker rose and walked to the fireplace, his coat tails folding back like wings as he stood staring at the flames. "She came from the woods with the rest of her marauding pack," he said acrimoniously, "ghouls, drawn to the scent of the crypt, or so I reckon, where my mother and I had only the day earlier laid my father within, clad in his black and violet robes. His protracted illness had rendered him an invalid for the last several years of his life. With my mother forty-five winters on, my younger sister dead, I only a boy and no servants to assist us, the castle was already in a state of desuetude. After Father's passing we withdrew to this level, which offered a better vantage and was more secure in the event of an outsider breaching our doors. Here we sequestered ourselves, and here I have since remained.

"It had been a prolonged and desperately bitter winter, and our provisions were as scarce as the flesh on our bones. Despite it being only the two of us, my mother nonetheless pronounced the funeral rites in old Clænish in the torch-lit vault. I can recall shivering beside her while the evil smell of my father's body surrounded me like a shroud. She seemed impervious to the latter as she recited the sacred words in a sullen and grim cadence. When it was time for the Passing On of the Lychstone, she took my hand and raised it over my father's chest. Her grasp was decidedly without tenderness, hard and cold, her nails drawing blood and though I cried out she did not release me until her arcane chanting had ended and the stone was taken from my father's neck and placed around her own.

"The next morning when I woke she was not in our chamber. After a frantic search of our diminutive suite of rooms, I found her in the northern tower. She was in a state of nervous terror. I joined her at the narrow lancet which looked out over the courtyard and the entrance to the crypt. The door there was opened slightly; as I watched, out from the gap appeared a rangy white wolf with an arm in its jaws. I recognized at once the shreds of violet in which it was wrapped.

"The beast dropped its pillage on the flagstones and commenced ripping away the flesh in ragged swathes, the fingers twitching as it tore. As it chewed, another figure appeared from behind the door. It was a young girl. Her hair was a sordid tangle; so starved and gaunt was she that she seemed a skeleton covered in flesh. She walked like the wolf and carried in her mouth her own meager plunder of meat. She was trailed by a smaller form, an incomprehensible amalgamation of the two figures feasting on the corpse of my father. Mother and child crouched near the male; he became still and growled menacingly, and so they moved off to another section of the courtyard. There the girl ripped off and devoured small bits, while the groveling mutation leapt and begged beside her. She offered none to the pup, even batted it cruelly into the brambles where it yelped and whined and thereafter remained, shivering and waiting for any scraps that might be left. Ere long the weather turned and a tempest moved in from off the sea, forcing the wretched family below. It was then that my mother told me that she must go down into the crypt.

"I thought she had gone mad with grief. I said that Father would never have us endanger ourselves for the sake of his remains. This she affirmed, stating that it was another obligation, one of paramount necessity, which compelled her thither. I begged her not to leave as she put on her cloak and tucked a large blade within its folds. She knelt, took off the necklace of black stone and put it around my neck. She closed her eyes, placed her fingers upon my forehead and whispered something brief and in the tongue of the Rook. When she looked upon me again it was with grave solemnity, and I knew that I had become its keeper. Lifting it in my palm, I pondered my reflection on the oily surface. My visage seemed to sink beneath into its depths the longer I stared.

"'It is the dark which no light can pierce,' she said. 'The black which piles above our beloveds, obscuring them from the lie of the stars. It is finality incarnate, a repellent of illusion and enchantment. It will always show you Truth. You must never remove it, for to do so would mean vulnerability to iniquity and falsehood.'"

"I whimpered, I pleaded. She struck me, then gripped my arms so tightly I cried out in shock, for neither she nor my father had ever before used physical violence upon me.

"'There are responsibilities larger than ourselves, Clive. You are but a boy, but this you must understand, and you must obey me now. Do not follow me, no matter what you hear or see, and should I not return, you must *not* come in search of me. You are henceforth the Eye of your fathers.'" She kissed me, firmly and in the same place that she had struck me. Then she clasped me to her—with such intensity I could hear her frantic heart thundering—released me, and was gone.

"I went to the lancet, grasping the stone for courage as I watched for her to appear below. Ere long I saw her: a tall and erect figure striding without faltering down the flagstones toward the entrance of the crypt. As she approached the door she withdrew the blade. She passed beyond the threshold into the blackness without hesitation, and I saw her not again."

Here the Caretaker paused and stared into one of the chamber's tenebrous corners where the fire shadows lapped like beating wings. "I did not remove my gaze from that doorway for the remainder of daylight. When by nightfall she had not emerged I quit my post and sank down with my back to the wall. Clasping the stone in my palm, I wept and brayed with the unalloyed intensity of a terrified boy of seven, for I knew unequivocally that I was alone. What was I to eat? How was I to live? I slept erratically, and at some late hour woke to a blinding glow too bright to be that of the waxing moon. I peered through the pointed slit, my arm raised to shield my eyes from the blaze concentrated there.

"What I saw was beyond logic. The girl stood with her back to the crypt entrance. She was no longer the vile creature I had seen squatting on the path. Her body was flawless and porcelain. Her hair rippled gently down her back as if it were alive, and her eyes were blank as a classical statue's. Her arms were outstretched before her, and cupped in her hands was an object from which light gushed in great tentacle-like streams. The entire courtyard was erumpent with it, curlicues of golden radiance spinning and swirling along the walls and the walkway. Everything it touched was restored. It whitewashed the bleeding lines of black mold from the ancient stone and reanimated the brown and crackled ivy to the lustrous green of the previous season. It scrubbed the grit from the corroded flagstones, restoring them to their subdued and noble bronze. It even built things which had not previously existed. A fountain in the shape of a rearing wolf was raised at the center of the garden, the low walls of its pool and the statue solidifying slowly and hardening to stone like a molten sword cooling from just out of the forge. Fantastical and wondrous as this was, my terror was amplified by what I heard coming from the light itself, for it had a most definite sound. *It was screaming!*"

I thought of the disembodied pleas beneath the water in the bath. I heard the fading dirge in the great hall as I guided my father through the dimmed expanse after the performance on our first night at the castle. I saw the faces splayed on the walls of Daeva's room, flattened as if pressed under incalculable weight and yet still sentient and alert. Ravis had paused briefly in his oral recounting, as if the weight of his own appalling memories were too crushing to give further air, and when he recommenced it was in a noticeably breathless tone.

"I dashed under the bed. For a long while I heard nothing. I thought that she had gone off. This was of course a foolish delusion. I heard the doors thrown back and then footsteps in the hall. She had been exploring the castle, and had reached the third floor. I curled more tightly in my hiding place, squeezing the stone in my shaking hand.

"Then ... something curious happened. My fear was suddenly supplanted by feelings of indignation and rage. I was infuriated and aggrieved at the treatment of my father's remains and the loss of my mother, and fired with a grim impulse to avenge them and protect my home, even if it meant my own demise. I heard my mother's voice in my mind, repeating: 'You are the Eye of your fathers.'

"I crawled from under the bed and swept the dust from my clothing. A stench of rot reached the little apartment as the footsteps drew near. I went out to meet them.

"I had expected the girl but found the wolf instead, standing not ten feet from me. Its formerly dingy coat was pure and unsullied as fresh snow, and its eyes were bright as sunlight reflected in a mirror. I took a step toward it, my heart thundering objection. It lowered its head and ... *grinned* at me. I swear it! The wolf advanced—its facile prey within leaping distance. I did not move. A feeling was gathering in me—or perhaps emptying me—I could not settle on which, as there seemed to be widening in my gut at the place where the stone lay; an expanding grave-black chasm larger than myself, and yet the nothing within it was like a mass pressing at the borders, stretching them until I thought I would burst were it not released.

"I held my arms out at my sides and felt the darkness extend from them like black feathers—indeed, it felt as though they were massive wings. I thrust them forward and the dark was flung like sheets of night, obscuring the walls and ceiling and floor with a single beat. The wolf was cloaked instantly, and I saw it again *as it was:* its ensanguined jaws, the scabby hide with its shard-like hackles, its muted lightning stare beneath which I beheld the snarling and ravenous resolve of a famished predator. Just as soon had I observed this did the wolf's ferocity diminish. It retreated backward a few paces, whining, and then turned and fled, that anguished light trailing it as if being dragged, and since that day neither wolf nor the girl has set foot here. Thus, I have been afforded the protection and the time to sift the letters, deeds, maps, charts of accounts, scrolls, and diaries scrawled by the hands of my hallowed ancestors, and author the first comprehensive biography of my family and our tottering dynasty."

"Then the stone is a shield," I said, "a repellent of that particular Light."

"Think of it rather as the remover of gleam from false jewels," the Caretaker replied.

I considered this, though only for a moment, for there was a detail which was far more perplexing at present than the workings of the aforementioned pair of enigmatic charms. "Just to be clear, Mr. Ravis. You are claiming that the girl in your tale is the same whom I know by the name of Daeva."

"Yes," said he.

"This you affirm, seemingly insensible to the implausibility, nay the *impossibility* of what you are implying."

One of the tapers on the desk expired. Ravis replaced it and, striking a match, lit the new candle. In the flare of flame my eye was drawn to something amidst the reams of parchment. It was a specific color; a particular shade of indigo which like a burning fuse leading to a bomb did not detonate in my mind for some time henceforth.

"I assure you, I am in possession of my full faculties of reason," the Caretaker said as he retook his seat. "And I have already explicated to you how the gem works, and therefore all that is necessary in comprehending the method by which she deludes as well as maintains the illusion of agelessness—she, in semblance a girl of fifteen despite the passage of nearly *forty-five years.*"

I was without words. Ravis, taking devious pleasure in my silence, said:

"It would be munificent of me to provide you with more detail. Shall I describe the lumbering, shriveled thing with which you have had dalliances these past several days? 'She' with whom you have confided, embraced, rutted?"

"*That will do,* Mr. Ravis!" I said sharply. I closed my eyes and placed my hands upon my forehead. I was dizzy to the point of nausea. I had to escape that cloistered room with its stink of musty pages and sour bed linen. I managed to maintain balance as I pushed myself forward, gained my feet and started toward the door. Ravis was there as I staggered out into the corridor, gripping my arm and turning me toward him.

"You cannot get it back without me," he said flatly.

I pulled away. "I am going to look for my *father.*"

"You will not find him on your own," he called after. "You *need* me, Jonas!"

My head was athrob, my stomach a knotted tangle. Enervated, I stumbled several times during the course of my retreat, scuffing knee and shoulder on damp stone. The further I walked, however, the greater became my stamina. The pounding in my head lessened, that churning ball of warm yarn in my gut unfurled and the queasiness dissipated. These pains were replaced by a deadened sensation in limb and torso. It was a curiously numbed and wooden feeling—I can conceive of no other way to describe it—and yet I felt as though I could pass through any impediment, be it blizzard or lava flow, gale or sea surge, sailing like sound, unhitched as it were to the tangible elemental world.

The door at the end of the passage opened into one of the turrets. I recognized it at once as the same in which I had found myself trapped not three days earlier. I descended the winding stair to the second level; there was no door hinged to the lancet opening as before, and what I saw through it was not the lavish hall leading to my chamber, but a half collapsed expanse of weather blasted limestone and buckling walls with gaping arches. I traversed the failing floor to my room and crossed dazedly over the threshold. The orange glass of the arched window had evaporated, leaving only the central stone mullion and its upper bifurcations. The furniture and tapestries were ragged and water damaged. The bed was sodden and stained as coffin silk, the shreds of fabric hung from the canopy like dead hair. The mattress appeared to have spawned innumerable generations of mice. As I regarded it I tried in vain to refute the ghastly reality that for several nights *I had actually slept there.* The chairs with their bloated cushions stood where they had for centuries before the barren hearth. One of the wardrobe doors gaped open, their mirrored doors tarnished and bleary. I went to it, peering in at the antiquated brittle dresses and faded slippers. Among these were other objects anachronous to the style of the garments hanging therein—piles of contemporary eye glasses, pocket watches, lockets, combs, hair pins, cuff links, and cameos amongst more valuable items like rings and necklaces, jeweled brooches and golden chains. They had been tossed there as afterthoughts, these artifacts from individuals whose lives had been cruelly taken. Their assassin was not there at present, but she had been quite recently. The bitter tang of the "Lovers' Tongues"—tangles of desiccated ivy strung along the canopy of the bed—and the stink of wolf clung to the bedclothes, potent as the invisible fug of must.

It is not what it appears. Miss Saffrey's words had been honest and axiomatic, and still I had not *seen,* nor perhaps had I really *believed*— distracted by my own arrogance and self-delusion. But there were no more stratagems left to entertain: Daeva had let fall the façade as she gathered to her everything that would be needed to draw out what she had sought from the moment she dispatched that erroneous letter of commission.

I fled the room and dashed back down the corridor. As I descended the final set of stairs I had a sudden and terrible foreboding, accompanied by a vision of the dress and alterations shop. Snow blew through the open door into the ransacked interior, lifting the hems of skirts and rippling the torn drapes. The window glass was punctured, the sewing table toppled onto its side. Something had fallen, or been dragged, down the stairs; the banister was knocked crooked, the stairs splintered, the dowels cracked like broken ribs.

Surveying this mentally caused me to falter physically. I reeled blindly through the doorway leading into the ground-level chamber where I skidded and collapsed. Lifting my face from the slime-glazed stone, I stared at the yellow-grey light filling the portal where the front door had been. There were no mirrors, no endlessly reflected candle flames in the foyer. Sections of the ceiling lay in moldering heaps on the floor, and pervading the space was the stink of animal feces. Along the western wall, partly illumined by the dirty light, I spied an assemblage of figures posed in an unmistakable arrangement.

I got to my feet and moved slowly toward them, creeping despite their eternally still visages, their glass eyes and stuffed constructions.

The dolls were seated in a large toy amphitheater, all facing the stage upon which stood a crude carved piano and bench. Most of the puppets were threadbare and rotted, like scarecrows left tied to their stakes a season too long. In the front row was a finely dressed trio. The Count in his baroque garb had been placed rather upright. His "flesh" had a dulled olivine tinge, as if carved from raw chrysolite. I recognized the Countess Marlena by her heterochromian eyes, one green and one yellow. The seat beside her was empty, and the next occupied by the Duke of Danesfall, his features literally chiseled into his wooden face, his eyeholes stuck with citrine stones. Nowhere amidst this farce did I discover any trace of my father, though beyond the stage I saw my bow snapped in twain, and a few paces from this, the viola lying face down in the shadows.

I gathered it like a lost child into my arms, my tears falling upon the satin black of that cherished and unblemished countenance. All else was forgotten: the shock of the ruin, Daeva, Clive Ravis' story, Isadora Saffrey. Even my father. I plucked lovingly each of the four strings, savoring their perfect song. I touched the scroll to my lips, calmed by the electric thrum of that familiar and intimate communion. Indeed, so enthralled was I by my beloved that I was but vaguely conscious of the light beginning to seep into the room like water.

"We are so alike, you and I...."

I heard the voice before I saw its speaker. Still on my knees, still embracing the viola, I turned, raising an arm to guard my eyes from Daeva, an ethereal monster wreathed in a halo of white light. She was statue-like, her skin milk glass, and her eyes unreal things: two golden beams with huge dilated irises black as grave pits. Her long, blade-like locks floated out from her head, moving gently, steadily, like weeds in an underwater current. Beneath the iridescent folds of her gauzy dress I saw Ida Saffrey's iron-thread necklace, its serpentine strands rooted into her flesh and enveloping a burning core where blazed the Cold Flame like a sliver of sun. The glow seemed to buoy her, for her feet hovered several inches off the stone floor.

"Performing what needs to be performed and protecting what must be protected, even as you know that it is scraping your cavity clean. I know of such responsibility, such vulnerability. We could have borne our burdens together, Jonas, shared immortality together, and eternal ecstasy. Our children would have possessed powers unlike any mortal who has ever walked in this life. And you, the sire of a new super-race, would have been king. *A king,* Jonas—the jester no longer. Instead you remain the Fool, the *maestro* of nothing save deception."

So absurd was the irony I found myself laughing. "Deception, yes," I said, gesturing at the surroundings. "Perhaps we *should* bind ourselves here and now, in this pilfered ruin. Where shall the altar be? Shall we first gain the consent of your wood and wax mother and father?"

Daeva narrowed her eyes, the twin beams honed to cutting edges. She began to float toward me; I scuttled backward, tucking the viola under my coat. "But now the idea of us together cools," she purred darkly. "That seamstress told you her lies and you embraced them. You brought *your* lies to my bed and embraced me. For that I will have my vengeance."

At those words, I felt an impervious shadow envelop my heart. "Where is she, Daeva?"

"Ah! How quickly grave he turns at her mention. Do you think that form with which you are so besotted will remain as supple and pliant as it is now? The body is a tomb, Jonas. It shrivels and decays while we yet occupy it, and we are made to accept that grim march, witnesses of our own extinction. Well, I *will not accept it!*"

Her words filled the room like a thunderclap, shaking the walls. They rained small bits of stone and mortar and dislodged a great chunk of masonry from the ceiling. The latter plummeted with such speed I had only an instant to throw myself out of its path before it crashed with splitting force onto the stone. Anger lit through me like a flare burst, obliterating fear. It was unnerving, this instantaneous shift of mood, as if someone else's feelings had been superimposed over my own. I was again filled with that radiating cold and constraining chill as that caliginous essence transposed itself to me from the inert body I clutched against my own. The flow of my blood slowed, cooled, congealing rivers running to my largo heart. A tenebrous veil descended over my vision; I was again usurped, seeing with the eyes of the implacable eidolon. I recalled the sensation of churning in my gut and knew it then not as yarn but hair, *her* hair, black as the will of the man who had tried to enslave her for eternity. I held the viola before me, and in that moment both saw and felt nothing but an empty shell in my hand, unresponsive to anything so abstract as love, vacated by its occupant in order to fortify the form containing its quarry.

Daeva was rising—several feet above the floor was she, and almost unobservable, surrounded as she was by an aura bright as a voltaic arc. The void-like portals of her eyes widened, and so too did her smile, exposing teeth gleaming like the new headstones of infants. Between light and dark then stood I: the inheritor of a curse, a pretender, and an instrument myself. I glanced at the Inamorta, dangling lifeless in my grasp, and in that moment I knew at last how to be free of it.

I let it slide until the scroll caught in my fingers. Clenching that clenched hand in my outstretched arm, I retreated a few paces until I felt the wall at my back, and then I swung. The viola shattered like a brittle skull; an explosion of yew and ebony and bone. Within me the phantom lurched and wailed, its moan rising in my throat like a belch. The white flash struck me an instant later—a blast of incinerating ice. I felt again that separation, same as I had in Daeva's room, though this time it was *Her* being drawn out. An amorphous cloud thick and black as coal smoke roiled from me, taking shape as it repelled, or perhaps consumed, the Light. She was the minor key personified; a *furioso* encore performance of stringy hair and gaping holes and bombazine wisp, blotting out the world wherever she raged. The enduring shroud that was Melania Morturia rose, flapping along the ceiling like a disoriented bat, and then shot toward the yellow-grey glow filling the equilateral arch where it hovered for several seconds. As it gradually dispersed so too did the voice of the Inamorta, fading like the final note of a long and mournful passage.

A scream behind me slashed the brief ensuing silence. I turned, anticipating Daeva, and instead saw Clive Ravis with an arm locked around her throat. In his other hand was a long blade which he was using to cut loose the writhing strands of the necklace. Daeva flailed and howled, raking his face with her nails and opening mean gashes on his cheeks but Ravis, intent in his work, barely flinched as he carved through her crackling flesh until at last the Cold Flame came free and Daeva flopped to the floor, unmoving.

The Caretaker peeled back the silver strands encasing the gem and with unabashed disgust discarded the limp arachnid form. He wiped the black ichor from the Cold Flame with gentle assiduousness and at last fitted it within the socket beside the Lychstone. The change was immediate and fearsome to behold. His threadbare suit was restored to sumptuous satin, the coattails curving inward like wing tips. His hair became glossy, styled as if by an invisible hand. Vivid amber steadily replaced the murky, well-bottom shade of his eyes. There was no amity to be found therein.

"A stellar performance, *maestro*," Ravis said. "Word of your mastery preceded you of course, though I had not known whether to anticipate cunning or caution. Not for a moment had I envisaged such utter buffoonery. Nevertheless, the task is done."

It was then that I reconciled the color of those particular pages on his desk with their lavender familiar, received by me at the royal palace a fortnight from that very date. "You sent the letter. It was *you* who commissioned us."

"And through you lured a singular object powerful enough to distract her. Now, with the property of my forefathers regained, I shall commence in restoring their once formidable abode and that pathetic village, and the name of Ravis shall again command reverence and awe in this region."

"Have you learned nothing?" I ejaculated, my eyes alighting momentarily on the gem. It appeared fainter than it had when Daeva had worn it, a mere pale yellow. "It will *consume* you, Clive, and you will end as your ancestor, mad and chained and shrieking in the dark!"

"You have forgotten, Mr. Layne. I am the Caretaker, and the last of my kin. None remain who might oppose me."

I said: "Then I will impede you no longer, beyond this one last inquiry. Where might I find my father?"

"'Shrieking in the dark,'" was his soft reply. Ravis tented his fingers over the necklace, then slowly parted them. The air around him began to pulsate as if it contained heat waves. An arc of thin and blinding radiance like the rim of an eclipse encircled him. The shadow it constrained boiled within; oviparous plumes escaped like solar flares and took the form of ragged flying forms as they were borne upon the air. They rose, gaining in both solidity and balance as they hovered, and ere long began diving toward me, their seemingly incorporeal beaks tearing my coat and uprooting thatches of my hair.

I fled aimlessly, screaming as the avian bombardment rained ceaselessly upon me. At length I fell, enveloped in a squawking cocoon of wings and talons. I covered my face as the rest of me was pecked and pulled, until at last I screamed no longer and sank to the floor, hoping then only for a swift ending of the pain.

It came, though not in the manner I had expected, for the flock suddenly evaporated. I became aware of a separate struggle on my left, and looking then in that direction saw the great white wolf with its jaws locked on the throat of Clive Ravis. The latter's eyes were the apotheosis of shock as he swung feebly at the beast, his fists having no impact on the creature. Despite my injuries I found myself rising and lumbering toward them. On my way I picked up the blade Clive had used upon Daeva. As I approached, the wolf jerked its head and the Caretaker of Blackspeak Castle, last of the line of the Rook, moved no more.

Releasing its kill, the wolf turned then to me, its ensanguined maw widening to a rictus. The shade of its eyes, like the gem, was weaker than it had been previously though the malevolence remained. There is no way of describing its gaze other than to say that it was a decidedly *human* malice I perceived in its stare. I could only ponder what wretched soul or combination of cutthroats, savages, and depraved rakes enlivened the beast. It lowered its head, arched its back, and as it lunged I offered the blade, firmly and without faltering, and with not a little surprise at my own dexterity, watched as it passed through the jaws and impaled the wolf through the brain.

Once my heart and breathing had regained their regular cadences, I crossed the delta of blood and removed the necklace from the corpse of Clive Ravis. The cord had been severed in the attack; after wiping it clean, I stowed it in my pocket. I had inferred from the Caretaker's rather unambiguous hint concerning the whereabouts of my father that he was in the place I had seen in my dream some nights earlier. And so I started through the ruin toward the rear of the castle, passing through a series of dim chambers which were hideously damp and reeking of urine. The last of these I recognized as the "great hall" where we had dined on our first night.

It was now a roofless shell. The long table and chairs stood in a square of tall grass. Brown water filled the stemware, and webs festooned the tarnished arms of the chandelier which had crashed on to the table decades earlier. I saw the chairs in which we had sat, and the meal of decaying leaves, bird carcass, and mouse droppings of which we had partaken. As I regarded this my vision began to blur and darken. I reached for the back of my former chair; it snapped off in my grasp and I was pitched sideways into the weeds. Vertiginous, I rose unsteadily and staggered through a hole in the wall in the direction of the overgrown courtyard.

The partitions and pathways were covered in snarls of vine and scrub. No stone wolf rose from the center of the dry fountain bed, no Lovers' Tongues made redolent the biting sea air with their seductive scent. Stepping through the brambles, I saw the tumulus arcing above the rear wall, and then the iron gate and the door with the rook carved upon it in low relief that led inside.

The gate was partly opened; it produced no squeal or groan as I pulled it back, which suggested to me that it was utilized with some frequency. I ducked inside and approached the inner door, before which I stood for several minutes attempting to discern how it might be breached, for there was no knob of any sort, and the slab itself was ponderous and unyielding. At length, I began to focus solely on the symbol engraved there, tracing the rook and the faceted gem with my fingers. The latter appeared in both size and design identical to the original. Curious, I drew the Cold Flame from my pocket and pressed it within. The door began sliding back at once, grinding in its ruts, and stopping only when it had fully recessed into the wall. A stench curled up from the depths—one unmistakable and eliciting a sense memory from my nightmares. The dissipating daylight penetrated only far enough to illumine a low and vaulted brick arch and the first three steps of a subterranean staircase which commenced a few paces from the threshold. A torch stood in a bracket beside the entrance and a flint striker hung below it. I removed these, and after several attempts was successful in producing enough sparks to set the brittle kindling aflame. It burned steadily and without haste. Once I was satisfied with the stability of this light source, I began to descend.

With each step the air grew colder and fouler. This was an old place, an ancient one, even, but the smell was not. Fresh decay pervaded there. Reaching the bottom of the stairs, I paused and raised the torch. My breath was visible in these depths. My flesh needled as I stared down an endless low and arched passage, though not due to the cold. *Yes, I have visited here,* I thought. I knew that I must proceed with care, for one could become easily disoriented in such tunnels, and thus hopelessly lost.

I started onward slowly, thrusting the light into the chambers as I walked. Within the dusty alcoves were the bones and crumbling coffins one would expect; that is to say, I saw nothing which provided substance to exemplify the stench which seemed to multiply in intensity the further I shuffled through the dark. This was, however, my only guide, and I determined then to follow it in whichever direction it seemed to worsen.

Thus I progressed, initially along the primary corridor, then making a series of turns which brought me deeper into the labyrinth and, alas, away from the only exit known to me. While navigating these convolutions I heard what I thought were footsteps, though I could not ascertain whether they were my own or something following me, keeping an intentional distance. Glancing at the torch, I became further alarmed by how much had been consumed—far more indeed than I had surmised would.

The first color, when I came upon it, was so bright against the homogeneous grey stone that it actually startled me. I crouched and examined the object: a shredded band of blue silk, stiff with dried blood. My eye was next drawn to something in my periphery lying adjacent, this a woman's black boot. I stood, held the flame aloft, and surveyed then what resembled a battlefield of mussed garments far as the light illumined. I stepped over these as if they were bodies, and indeed some of the severed sleeves and breeches *still covered limbs*. Peering at these, I saw that they had not merely been torn—most were also *bitten*, or had flesh missing as the result of a bite. They were heaped like drifted snow; thicker became these piles—as did the infernal stench, which rendered the air almost irrespirable and which seemed to permeate my very flesh—as I reached the end of the corridor, where I was surprised to see a door and, propped against it, the battered and still form of Isadora Saffrey.

I pushed through the clog of remains, beckoning to her all the while and receiving no reply. She had been abducted from her bed, or such did her filth-streaked nightgown suggest. Her hair was a snarled veil, partially obscuring her visage which was swollen and blackened with bruises. I touched that face and found it to be the worst sort of cold, and yet, pressing an ear to her chest I heard the faintest of thrums. I took her hand; the warmth of my own caused her to stir. The eye which was not inflamed opened slightly and looked at me.

"I am here, Miss Saffrey," I said. I sensed no recognition in her gaze, though this was difficult to determine with certainty given her condition and the low light, for the torch was rapidly diminishing: to my consternation I observed I had but minutes before it expired. Turning toward the passage on my right, I stepped just within the arced opening and held up the fading flame. How is one to describe the horrors it disclosed? Though the details persist in my memory with abhorrent and maddening infallibility, I shall herein render them only in sketches, lest the reader of this chronicle find seated in his consciousness visions which are concurrently exceedingly depraved and plaintive and consequently irremovable from one's mind.

I have already detailed the noxious intensity of rot and decay; here, alas, was its wellspring. The dead lined the walls on either side of the passage, posed sitting upright with their legs stretched before them. Some of the livid or gnawed upon or putrefying heads rested on the shoulders of their neighbors while others sat rigid and fleshless, mouths and eyes gaping eternally in the dark. At the center of this macabre congress was a stinking circular mass of jackets and petticoats and taffeta and worsted trousers and the like. The faces of the Missing from the counting house wall crowded my brain like phantoms. I imagined their families seeking them in vain, and now I scanned the ravaged countenances, seeking out my own.

At length, I located my father, set alongside the others. I was able to recognize him only by his hands. As I looked at them a nascent memory—perhaps it was even my very first—came to me of watching those same hands running left to right down the keyboard. I was sitting beside him on the bench, eyes level to the keys. I could recall thinking while observing that flurry of notes that he was in possession of magic, or indeed *possessed by it*. Completing the scale, he summoned me then to play; he regarded me as if I were a fascinating animal as I raised a finger and depressed the second A from middle C. The ringing note was to me bright as a beam of sun in a root cellar. He then took my hand and guided me through a simple melody.

I hummed that same tune through heavy sobs as I took his cold hand in mine. So weakened was I by grief, as well as my own wounds, that I was no longer bothered by the shrinking torchlight. The fumes and faces of death became less appalling. It was right, I thought, to die here, for I had nothing. I turned then and looked back at the girl, and that was when I saw it gazing at me from the mouth of the passage.

The grotesque fruit of its mother and father's bestial copulation was something like a paused collision. It crouched crookedly in shadow, one hind leg bare and knee-toward, the other of stifle and hock in form. It was unequivocally male. The torso was lupine, though distorted by a severely arced spine and the upper arms of a man. The hands consisted of only partially articulated digits. The ashy pelt was a scabrous amalgam of flesh and fur, scratched raw perhaps from lice, perhaps from ennui. It shivered continuously, though in an oddly controlled manner, as if the condition—the reaction to the perpetual chill—had become part of its physiology, and yet the human half of its intuition had instinctively pulled on a tattered frock coat pilfered from one of its "companions." As in the dream, it regarded me with coin-like eyes. But other than the dying torchlight reflected in them, I saw nothing of peril; rather the nameless aberration seemed to cower in the alien glow and grow anxious and tentative. It raised the canine rear leg and scratched its human ear, then made a sound—a ghastly parody of speech—which began as a canine yowl and concluded in a low and incomprehensible, though discernibly *syllabic*, murmur. This sequence repeated threefold, the final utterance with the unmistakable lilt of dismay and frustration. I thought: He is trying to communicate with me. He has recognized and is appealing to my innate compassion. He wants to call me *friend*.

I looked at the reverently displayed dead—the scraps he had been tossed to feed upon, and had in his isolation, befriended. I looked at the miserable pile of clothing at my feet, and now it occurred to me that it was arranged *nest-like*. He slept there, amongst them—familiars who, if not to see, he could at least hold in the infinite dark. He leaned down and tenderly began to lift Miss Saffrey. Roused by his touch, she opened her eyes, and beholding the incomprehensible form clasping her, let out a chaffed scream. I yelled: *Stop!* The creature looked at me, his eyes the only illumination as the torch dimmed, flickered, and crackled out.

Without deciding to, I found myself reaching in my pocket and removing from it the gem. A fissure had developed down its center; it continued to emit light, though now of a sickly white yellow hue which leaked rather than poured. This muted sheen fell like smog obscured moonlight on the creature which, upon seeing the faceted object—the embodiment of its imprisonment—dropped the seamstress, let out a feral bellow, and charged.

In his gruesome gait the full corruption of his anatomy was exposed. Despite his deformities he did not lack speed; indeed, so sudden was his reaction that I had only an instant myself to react. It was the recognition of the shared attributes in those incandescent eyes and the gem itself which caused me to throw it, with all of the force that I could muster, to the floor.

Light exploded through the tunnel; so brilliant was the initial blast it left blotches of shadow in my vision for hours after. The creature was frozen mid-leap (how *close* it had been!) where for a few seconds he remained before the cold fire incinerated him into a heap of snowy ash. The light itself was transforming into figures, no longer smeared together but independent of one another. They glided through the passages, up the walls, along the ceiling, their radiance revealing every corroded and grime glazed inch of that dungeon as they sought a means of egress.

They accompanied me as I went to Miss Saffrey. She was limp and insensible as I gathered her and turned to the door. There was a knob at the center; it did not move, but there was give between wood and stone frame. Behind me I could feel the figures crowding, sensing escape. Combined, their individual chills paradoxically radiated a sort of heat and created pressure and I do not doubt that without their aid the door would not have given when I thrust my shoulder against it.

A pony trap lined with soggy straw partly obstructed the exit. I stepped beyond it while around me the light forms flowed, ascending and merging with a shell-burst hue of sunset visible through a gash in the collapsing roof. I recognized the room by its shelves though they were then empty. A warped desk, presumably the same on which I had penned part of this very narrative, stood before them. There was a table and a pair of upturned crates near the fireplace. Resting upon the latter's andirons was an abandoned crow's nest. I looked again at the trap—the last of a line of beds my father had occupied in the past decade—and wept at the bitter circumference; at where our ambition had in the end delivered us.

The woman in my arms stirred as I carried her out of the ruin. Her injuries were manifold and frightful to behold and I knew that hers would be a precarious convalescence, should she survive the night. I started through the rambling overgrowth surrounding the castle in the direction of the road leading back to the village. As I reached it I was arrested by a gurgling roar. Turning, I saw Daeva lurching from the maw of the derelict keep as if it were vomiting her out. She was a fantastical vision of horror. Her flesh was crackled and curdled and dropped off as she walked. Her head moved incessantly, eyeless yet seeking. Her mouth opened and closed fish-like, drawing breath in stertorous gasps. The hole where the gem had once nested was like a pistol blast, seeping black rivulets down her spoiled gown.

I knew what she sought. I laid the seamstress beside the path and moved toward the edge of the cliff. Holding the necklace in which the Lychstone was still encased, I raised it and beckoned her. The wrecked visage swiveled in my direction; she howled, and charged. I waited until she was nearly upon me, then turned and heaved the stone into the sea and Daeva followed it over.

I peered down at the rising tide lapping at the boulders. She lay upon one of these, her body split like a lobster tail. I watched as the waves dismantled her, piece by piece sinking into the fire-colored sea.

Epilogue

I returned to the castle one last time: to retrieve my father.

I came with the other families from Larmes Harbor, and together we claimed our dead. For six days trains of mourners could be seen moving up and down the hillside. The Found were carried back to the village and burned en masse near the harbor—including Theodore Layne, and Clive Ravis, whose body I removed myself rather than allow it to rot in the castle. I added the shards from the Inamorta to the pyre, but ground the bone adornments and gave them to the wind. The ash was shoveled into the sea.

Nine nights later Blackspeak Castle caught fire. It burned through the following day and smoldered for a week. No investigations were made with regards to the origin of the blaze. To-day the unvisited ruin resembles more a geological anomaly than a man-made edifice.

I repaired the damage to the alterations shop, re-ordered its contents, and slept on a cot downstairs during the subsequent weeks in which I cared for Isadora: boiling broth, emptying bedpans, changing bandages, and searching the village for Pendleton, who had alas gone missing. We spoke frequently and exhaustively on subjects prosaic and pensive and lachrymose, and retiring afterward to my little collapsible bed under the stairs, I was more contented and gained more rest than I had in all those regal chambers combined. In short, I found myself recovering as well.

One afternoon when I was returning from errands I saw the cat sitting on the stoop. He was lean and his fur clumped and knotted, but otherwise appeared without injury. He eyed me dubiously, even hissed at me when I approached, though when I opened the door he entered without hesitation. He located his mistress, who was most tearful at beholding him—and he nonplussed by her unwillingness to release him. His return did much in hastening in her recuperation. After I had procured for him a considerable dinner which he devoured to the last speck, he leapt onto Isadora's bed, curled up at her feet and did not move from the spot until the morning. That night I passed there with her as well, and have every night since.

Recently I bought from a local luthier a new viola. Rather than yew and bone, it is of the traditional maple and spruce—seventeen inches, pale-varnished. For months I had loathed the idea, and yet something within me that I thought had vanished with the Inamorta needed music. I desired to write it again, and to perform it. I thought about the children whom I had played for in the village square, and knew as well that I wanted to become a pedagogue.

The worst moment came just before raising the bow. Would I truly be able to play? Had it all been an illusion, false as the grandeur of Teethsgate? My doubts were manifold, and the potential despair which would result from those implications too harrowing to contemplate. At length, my courage returned, and when the hair bit the strings a song came. It was my song, my experience, *my voice,* made substantial through that tool of wood and wound gut. And as the notes flowed, tragic and triumphant and completely under *my* will, I knew there was nothing to fear.

It will take time to get used to that feeling.

Acknowledgements

This book has gone through many versions and alterations since the summer of 2011 when the first draft was completed. Therefore there are many to thank—in many capacities.

First, to the luthiers at Upton Bass String Instrument Company in Mystic, Connecticut: Gary Birkhamshaw, Jack Hanlon, Eric Rene Roy, and Tom Clark. I had the honor of working with these gentlemen for four years—learning the trade, the history of viol family instruments, and enjoying their good company. The technical aspects of this book are derived from these years, and I am forever grateful to them for their belief in me as an artist and individual. This book would not have been possible without them.

To the initial cold readers—Amy Brady, Fiona Fox, Mary Robles, and Suzi Weyer—for their input, advice, and encouragement. To John McIlveen at Haverhill House for considering the story in an earlier draft, and for suggesting edits which much improved the manuscript. To Curtis M. Lawson and Barry Dejasu for reading the book in its subsequent form and believing in it. To S. T. Joshi for editing (on two occasions!), and copyediting the book. Due to his considerable knowledge on period literature, the story has gained a great deal of verisimilitude in both language and style. Also, a huge thank you to S. T. for his estimable skill in music—he took a hummed recording of music that had been locked in my head for the past three years and put it down on paper. I am indebted to him for the transcription.

Finally—and *certainly* not least of all—thank you to Joe Morey and Bobbi at Weird House Press for believing in me as an author, and for producing such a beautiful volume. Working with Joe on this book and watching it come to fruition after all these years has been one of the true joys of my creative life, and I'm grateful to him for everything. A big thank you as well to F. J. Bergmann at Weird House for her keen editorial eye and thorough copyedit which saved me from looking a fool in many places. And thanks to Nick Greenwood for the absolutely incredible illustration/cover.

Love and thanks to my family, friends, teachers, and readers. And *Love* and *Endless Gratitude* to Mary Robles, for more reasons than could ever be listed here.

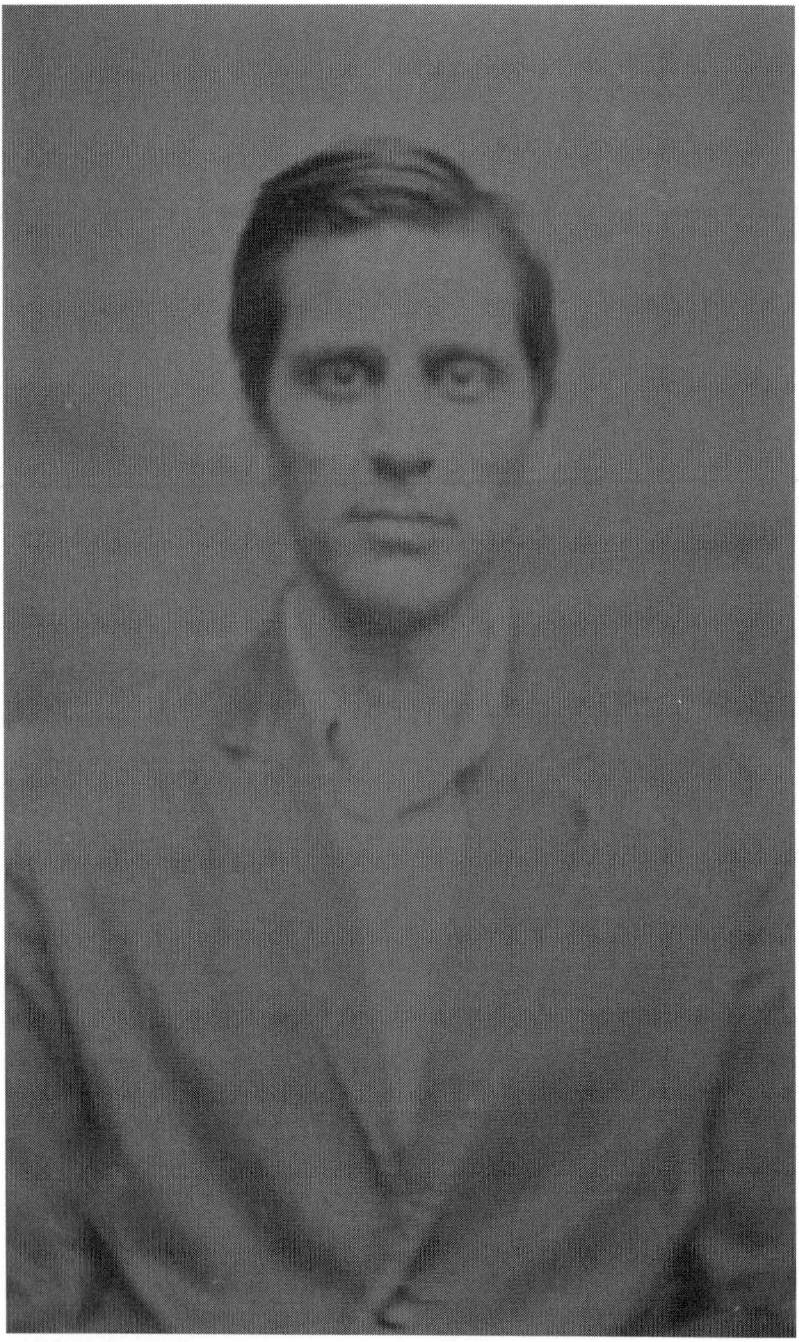

About the Author

Joshua Rex is an American author and historian. He was born in Sandusky, Ohio, and grew up between the Midwest and New England. He is the author of the novel *A Mighty Word* (Rotary Press) and the collections T*he Descent and Other Strange Stories* (Weird House Press) and *What's Coming for You* (Rotary Press), and hosts the podcast The Night Parlor where he interviews authors, artists, historians, and musicians.

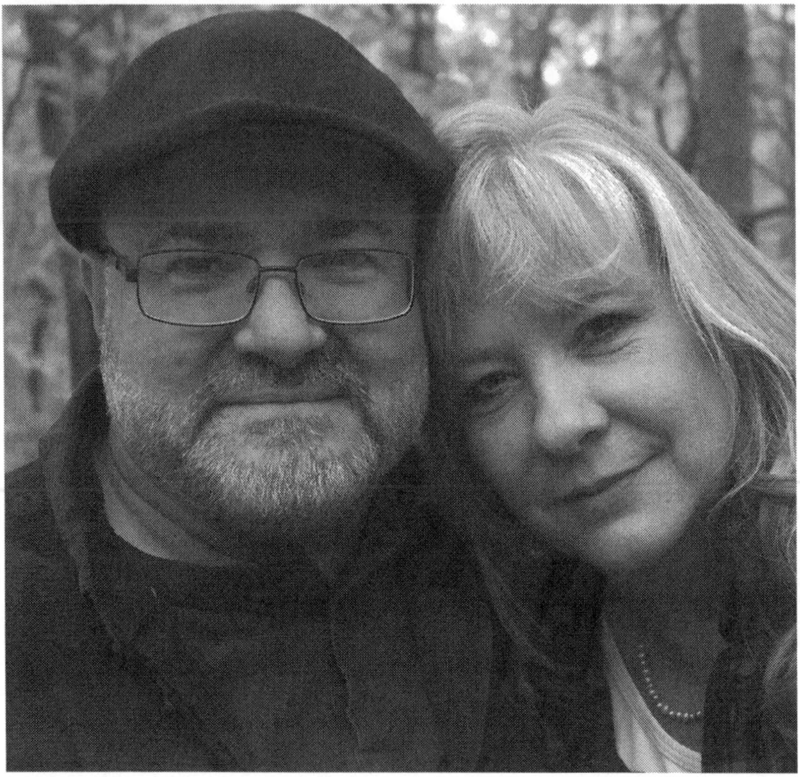

About the Artist

Nick Greenwood graduated from East Carolina University with a BFA in illustration. He has worked as an illustrator/concept artist/designer in the advertising, gaming, and publishing industries for over twenty years.

A brief list of clients include AT&T, Modiphius, Rubbermaid, Dias Ex Machina, Hardee's, IBM, Goodman Games, Green Ronin Publishing, Wyvern Gaming, and Poisoned Pen Press.

Nick lives in Jamestown, NC, with his wife of 30 years and is the father of four daughters, two dogs and a cat.

Made in the USA
Columbia, SC
04 November 2022